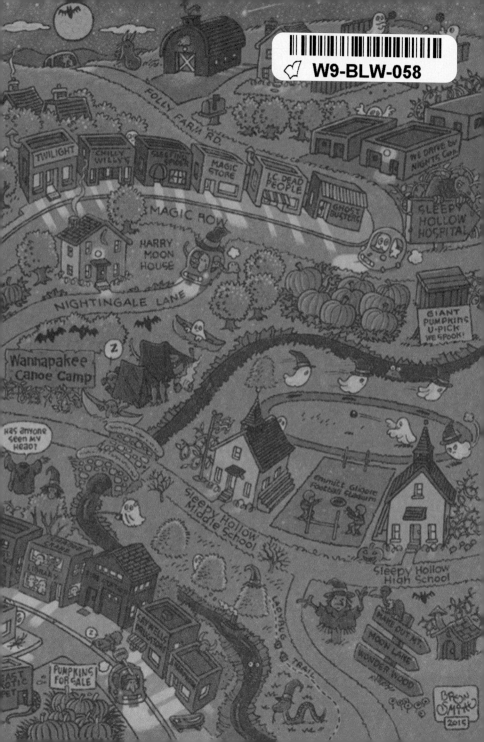

THE AMAZING ADVENTURES OF

HARRY MOON

SHOWDOWN ON NIGHTINGALE LANE

by

Mark Andrew Poe

Illustrations by Christina Weidman

with Becky Minor

rabbit publishers

Showdown on Nightingale Lane
by Mark Andrew Poe
© Copyright 2017 by Mark Andrew Poe. All rights reserved.

Rabbit Publishers
1624 W. Northwest Highway
Arlington Heights, IL 60004

Illustrations by Christina Weidman
Interior Design by Lewis Design & Marketing
Creative Consultants: David Kirkpatrick, Thom Black and Paul Lewis

ISBN: 978-1-943785-36-0

10 9 8 7 6 5 4 3 2 1

1. Fiction - Action and Adventure 2. Children's Fiction
First Edition
Printed in U.S.A.

"You have to grow small
before you can become great."

~ SAMSON

TABLE OF CONTENTS

H

PREFACE

Halloween visited the little town of Sleepy Hollow and never left.

Many moons ago, a sly and evil mayor found the powers of darkness helpful in building Sleepy Hollow into "Spooky Town," one of the country's most celebrated attractions. Now, years later, a young eighth grade magician, Harry Moon, is chosen by the powers of light to do battle against the mayor and his evil consorts.

Welcome to *The Amazing Adventures of Harry Moon*. Darkness may have found a home in Sleepy Hollow, but if young Harry has anything to say about it, darkness will not be staying.

FAMILY AND FRIENDS

Harry Moon

Harry is the thirteen-year-old hero of Sleepy Hollow. He is a gifted magician who is learning to use his abilities and understand what it means to possess the real magic.

An unlikely hero, Harry is shorter than his classmates and has a shock of inky, black hair. He loves his family and his town. Along with his friend Rabbit, Harry is determined to bring Sleepy Hollow back to its true and wholesome glory.

Rabbit

Now you see him. Now you don't. Rabbit is Harry Moon's friend. Some see him. Most can't.

Rabbit is a large, black-and-white, lop-eared, Harlequin rabbit. As Harry has discovered, having a friend like Rabbit has its consequences. Never stingy with advice and counsel, Rabbit always has Harry's back as Harry battles the evil that has overtaken Sleepy Hollow.

Honey Moon

She's a ten-year-old, sassy spitfire. And she's Harry's little sister. Honey likes to say she goes where she is needed and sometimes this takes her into the path of danger.

Honey never gives in and never gives up when it comes to righting a wrong. Honey always looks out for her friends. Honey does not like that her town has been plunged into a state of eternal Halloween and is even afraid of the evil she feels lurking all around. But if Honey has anything to say about it, evil will not be sticking around.

Sampson Dupree

Samson is the enigmatic owner of the Sleepy Hollow Magic Shop. He is Harry's mentor and friend. When needed, Samson teaches Harry new tricks and helps him understand his gift of magic.

Samson arranged for Rabbit to become Harry's sidekick and friend. Samson is a timeless, eccentric man who wears purple robes, red slippers, and a gold crown. Sometimes, Samson shows up in mysterious ways. He even appeared to Harry's mother shortly after Harry's birth.

III

Mary Moon

Strong, fair, and spiritual, Mary Moon is Harry and Honey's mother. She is also mother to two-year-old Harvest. Mary is married to John Moon.

Mary is learning to understand Harry and his destiny. So far, she is doing a good job letting Harry and Honey fight life's battles. She's grateful that Rabbit has come alongside to support and counsel her. But like all moms, Mary often finds it difficult to let her children walk their own paths. Mary is a nurse at Sleepy Hollow Hospital.

John Moon

John is the dad. He's a bit of a nerd. He works as an IT professional and sometimes he thinks he would love it if his children followed in his footsteps. But he respects that Harry, Honey and possibly Harvest will need to go their own way. John owns a classic sports car he calls Emma.

Titus Kligore

Titus is the mayor's son. He is a bully of the first degree but also quite conflicted when it comes to Harry. The two have managed to forge a tentative friendship, although Titus will assert his bully strength on Harry from time to time.

Titus is big. He towers over Harry. But in a kind of David vs. Goliath way, Harry has learned which tools are best to counteract Titus's assaults while most of the Sleepy Hollow kids fear him. Titus would probably rather not be a bully but with a dad like Maximus Kligore he feels trapped in the role.

Maximus Kligore

The epitome of evil, nastiness, and greed, Maximus Kligore is the mayor of Sleepy Hollow. To bring in the cash, Maximus turned the town into the nightmarish, Halloween attraction it is today.

He commissions the evil-tinged celebrations in town. Maximus is planning to take Sleepy Hollow with him to Hell. But will he? He knows Harry Moon is a threat to his dastardly ways, but try as he might, he has yet to rid himself of Harry's meddling.

Kligore lives on Folly Farm and owns most of the town including the town newspaper.

GREAT GOLD

Sleepy Hollow was a magical destination. People came from all over the world to experience the town where every day was Halloween night. Magic was the name of the game in Sleepy Hollow.

Anyone who wanted to be a truly awesome magician in that unusual little town needed a mentor. Harry Moon of Sleepy Hollow was a fortunate thirteen-year-old. He had three of them. "No one has friends like me," Harry would always say.

There was Samson Dupree, the eccentric proprietor of the Sleepy Hollow Magic Shoppe His shop had opened up, mysteriously enough, the day after the town went orange and black. Samson wore a weird golden crown on his head and always seemed to be filled inside with something or other, like a jelly donut. His jet-black hair resembled a stack of burnt pancakes. He wore a luxuriant cloak and red slippers. Sampson was always interested in spending quality time with Harry. Despite his peculiar ways, Harry found Samson quite wise about magic and life.

Then, of course, there was Harry's special rabbit friend who popped in and out of his top hat and generally was always around. While his name was indeed Rabbit, Harry suspected he wasn't really a rabbit at all. Harry appreciated that he seemed to be the only one able to see Rabbit, except for babies and mommies-to-be. It was also true that Rabbit never whispered a word to Harry that wasn't true.

Finally, there was the famous Elvis Gold. Elvis was one of the greatest illusionists in the world. He was a pop idol magic man. While Harry Moon considered Elvis his mentor in all things magic, Harry had never actually met the magician and probably never would. But no matter. Harry Moon was Elvis Gold's greatest fan and had been for years. Even today, Harry's first recollection of anything in his life was of the popular Elvis Gold Flashlight App.

Harry could not recall the first time he knew who his mom or dad or sister was. He could not remember the first time he met up with the family dog, Half Moon. But Harry Moon absolutely could tell you about his very first real-life memory. It was the shaft of light from the Elvis Gold Flashlight App. Harry could remember sitting in his playpen as a three-year-old and swiping his tiny finger over the app on his dad's cell phone. He remembered his surprise at the beam of light that emanated from the cell's lens, changing from white to red to emerald to blue.

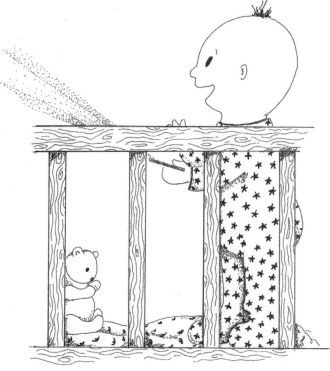

8

In his very first big boy bed, wearing his Superman pajamas, Harry Moon waved the shaft of light from the Elvis Gold Flashlight across the ceiling, filling the room with color. Before he ever went through the doors of kindergarten class, Harry Moon was already perfecting the art of the one-arm vanish magic trick, using the Elvis Gold Flashlight App as the magic beam that he would make appear and disappear with his sleight of hand. From almost the beginning of his journey with magic, Elvis Gold had captured Harry's heart.

For years, Harry Moon collected enough lawn mowing money to eventually buy an Elvis Gold magic set. He convinced his mom to order it for him over the internet. Every afternoon after school, Harry would hop off the Sleepy Hollow Middle School bus and rush to the mailbox, waiting for his *Elvis Gold's Amazing and Spectacular Magic Set for Ages Eight to Twelve* to arrive.

9

After four excruciating afternoons, rummaging through the mailbox and finding only crummy bills and cheaply-printed grocery advertisements, the fifth afternoon proved to be the charm. Harry looked out at the mailbox from the school bus window and let out an excited yelp. Alongside the mailbox, hanging from the red flag by a string was a majestic, brown cardboard box! Finally!

Harry Moon's heart was pounding out of his chest. He could barely breathe as he rushed down the steel steps of the bus and stumbled out to the curb. Harry ran toward the mailbox, his hands shaking.

He detached the package from the mailbox flag and brought it indoors. He placed it down on the round kitchen table and opened the box with the care and sacredness of a doctor on the operating table. Harry gasped out loud as he stepped back and stared at the *Elvis Gold's Amazing and Spectacular Magic Set* sparkling inside. It bore a shine as bright as the Flashlight App. The magic set was golden, with the heft and presence of a bar of gold bullion. From the picture on the box and in his signature golden bowler hat, Elvis Gold stared up at Harry with a wink. Elvis had piercing dark eyes, bright with mischief and rebellion. There was a tuft of black whiskers at his chin known as the "poet patch." Around his neck was a chain holding an amulet of purple and gold.

Harry gently pulled the cellophane off the golden box. With itching fingers, he took the top of the magic set and lifted it aside. In his imagination, he could never have known such a

10

treasure chest of wonder existed anywhere in the world. Inside was his very own trademark golden bowler hat of Elvis Gold. It, too, sparkled. Without a thought, Harry placed the golden hat upon his head. Feeling the weight of its magnificence, Harry could easily have been a prince or a king. In his bowler-crown, he gazed down at the package, noticing a cellophane pack containing Elvis' golden cape. He reached for it in a daze; everything within him seemed overly focused on his package, captive as if in some marvelous dream.

His fingers tore open the shrink-wrap that held the golden magician's cape. He peeled the cape from the wrap. Before he even realized it, there he was in the ordinary kitchen of his Sleepy Hollow home, transformed from a regular kid into his idol, Elvis Gold. Making the transformation complete, Harry Moon plucked his fingers inside the package and found the golden wand. With a swipe as natural as the swipe across his cell screen, Harry ran the wand through the air. He caught a glimpse of himself in the reflection of the family toaster and was amazed.

But he was not distracted by the comely golden figure of himself for long, for his eyes were drawn back to the box. Inside were the Elvis Gold playing cards and the plentiful silk scarves in gold and purple and red and green. There was a painted wooden "magic box" that could be used for any number of tricks. There were three plastic eggs that, when opened, might hold trinkets, scarves, and sponges which could expand or shrink depending upon the pressure applied. He was ready, with Elvis Gold's help, to become a real illusionist.

Harry's little sister, Honey Moon, entered the house from the kitchen door and studied her brother for a moment, her eyes narrowing into a squint.

"Harry Moon," she said in mock regard, "I am shocked!" She was so gob-smacked with his transformation that she stopped in her tracks, her school books frozen against her chest.

"I shocked you?" he asked.

"I never expected you to ever look so cool!"

12

"Cool?" he asked, looking once again into his reflection in the toaster oven. "You think I look cool?" He adjusted the brim of his sparkling bowler hat and played with the collar of his cape. He picked at his chin, imagining his poet's patch of whiskers—another signature of Elvis Gold. But, he was still a tad young for that to happen.

"Even though you have not reached puberty," said Honey, running her eyes over him from toe to head, "you have definitely transformed yourself. You look cool. When I first laid eyes on you, I thought you were a high school freshman."

"A freshman?" he asked, incredulously.

"A freshman," said Honey. "Maybe even a sophomore."

Harry looked again at his towering presence in the toaster oven. He sensed it, too. The bowler and cape made him more than he was. He was no longer just a kid living at the corner of Nightingale Lane and Maple

Sugar Road. He was looking like the great celebrity, known as "Great Gold" around the world for his astonishing illusions and magic.

Later, in his bedroom, Harry could not take his eyes off his reflection. In his cape and bowler, Harry Moon stood in front of the pine chest of drawers and stared at his likeness in the mirror. Harry could not remember the last time his sister had complimented him. He turned his head back and forth looking for what she saw in him and, indeed, as he stared, he found it. He had caught the glitter of Elvis Gold in his very self.

"That will get you into trouble," said Rabbit as he looked over at Harry while he lounged on Harry's twin bed. Rabbit would often just suddenly appear as if he were on stage popping out of a hat. But this was real life and Rabbit would just pop in. Well, at least, for Harry Moon.

"What will get me into trouble, Rabbit?"

"That attitude of yours," Rabbit sighed.

14

"Are we not supposed to love ourselves?" asked Harry.

"Love, yes. Adore, no."

"Adore?" Harry asked as he picked at his chin, believing he may have seen some hint of whiskers there. "You think I am adoring myself? I don't believe that's true."

"Adore. Yes, I am most certainly seeing that. Adore. Blinded love."

15

"I adore no one, Rabbit. Except perhaps Sarah Sinclair. And maybe, Elvis Gold. But I wouldn't say, 'adore." I would say 'idolize.'"

"Geesh," said Rabbit as he put his paw against his furry cheek, "you should just hear yourself talk." Rabbit was technically considered a Harlequin rabbit. He was a mix of black and white. His face looked like an ink bottle had exploded on it.

"He's a pretty good magician," said Harry Moon. "Elvis Gold is better than good. He is as good as it gets. Why should I not want to be as great as he is?"

"Because you need to be you, Harry. And you have what Elvis will never have. You have a rabbit who guides you. Me. You have real magic, not just pretend stuff."

Harry looked over at Rabbit who sat on the bed, leafing through the latest *People* magazine. He then looked back at his reflection in the mirror. He turned the golden brim of the sparkling bowler hat slightly on his head, adding even further coolness to himself. Harry sighed.

Walking over to his bed, Harry plunked himself down next to Rabbit.

"Yep, you are right, my friend," said Rabbit as Harry put his arm around him.

"Right about what?" asked Harry. Rabbit looked up at Harry with his furry harlequin face of white and black.

"Right about what you were thinking," Rabbit replied.

"And what was I thinking?" Harry asked.

"You were thinking that the really important things in life cannot be found in a box," said Rabbit. "You were thinking of your favorite book, *The Little Prince*, and that special line, 'That which is essential cannot be seen.' You were thinking that the important virtues in life like courage, loyalty, and kindness cannot be seen like your golden hat or your golden cape."

17

"Wow, you're good," said Harry with a smile. "I don't get how you are able to do that."

"I should be. I am Rabbit, after all."

Harry looked over from the bed into the mirror. He readjusted the shiny bowler on his head a third time.

"But Harry?"

"Yes, Rabbit?" Harry said.

"Just because you are thinking about the really important things in life," Rabbit added, "doesn't mean you are really believing it."

"Hmmmm," Harry said with a furrow in his brow.

"Oh yeah," said Rabbit, watching his friend's face. "It hasn't fully sunk in."

ELVIS IN THE JUNGLE

There is nothing better to make you feel small than attending a concert at the age of thirteen years old. Big-time concerts have huge crowds. There are crazy fans screaming and yelling. People are pushing and pulling and carrying on like fanatics. Everything at a concert can seem wild, uncontrollable, and larger than life.

Yet, Harry Moon had done the impossible. Harry had convinced his mom and dad that he was responsible enough to take the train into Boston and walk five blocks to the *Elvis Gold in the Jungle Event* at the AT&T Theatre. Simply unbelievable.

Before his parents drove him to the train station to take the Amtrak train into Boston, John Moon had a few words for his son.

"Harry, I hope you understand the magic that Elvis Gold performs on stage is sheer trickery," said John Moon.

"Trickery?" asked Harry.

"Absolutely. Illusion. He manipulates reality, but he does not change it. He is faking the audience out. He has no real power. It's all a trick."

"I get it, Dad. But he is still a genius. Nobody can figure out how he does it. Everyone thinks it's magic. That's why he is called a magician. Best in the world, Dad."

"But, you do *understand*, Harry, that he is a big quack. His magic is not real."

"You mean all smoke and mirrors?"

"Something like that. Harry, I know he is a great magician. But, by definition, he is a trickster. He's not really *doing* any of it. Let's face it. In the end, Elvis Gold is a phony. That's why they call him an illusionist. Do you remember when you were little and you wanted to put Harold Runyon's ghost in a Coke bottle? The man who saved my life in the war?"

"Yes. I haven't been able to figure that out yet..."

"Son, you'll never be able to do that. It's impossible. Maybe you could master it as an illusion, but no soul could ever fit in a bottle."

"I'm not so sure, Dad," said Harry as they walked toward the A train into the Boston Theatre District. "I think Solomon was able to do that with dark spirits."

"What are you saying?"

"Dad, Solomon had a whole room full of bottles and jars of dark spirits."

"Harry, why do you go on like this?"

"Because it's in the Book, Dad. Look it up." Harry gave his dad a hug and hopped onto the train's steps. "I'll be careful, pops. Tell mom not to worry. I got this."

22

For Elvis Gold, the *Elvis Gold in the Jungle Tour* had been a sensation. It had sold out in every venue across the world. Dressed only in a loin cloth, Elvis swung from vines and branches across the stage and into the theater. He produced lions, tigers, and giraffes from his sleight of hand. In the grand finale, he rode an elephant onto the stage, followed by a parade of other elephants.

"Boy, I can barely produce a rabbit on stage," thought Harry. He looked out the window of the train, whizzing past the suburban roads and fields of Sleepy Hollow toward the skyscrapers of Boston.

"Yes, but what a Rabbit," replied Rabbit as he gazed out at the changing landscape of the Amtrak window. Rabbit took the train whenever he could and absolutely would never miss the chance to tag along with Harry on his first trip to Boston. While Rabbit was invisible to most, Harry could quite clearly see him sitting next to him and appreciated his presence on this particular trip immensely.

"I AM grateful to have you as part of my magic, bunny boy," said Harry.

"Sometimes having a rabbit is enough," said Rabbit.

"You know I love you, Rabbit. But sometimes having only a rabbit does not seem to be enough."

"You want what you don't have. I understand. You want lions and giraffes. But always remember, it is all there for you already. You must use me to become better. Even real magic requires practice. Didn't you just talk about the connection between practice and success in school?" asked Rabbit.

"I know, I know. The Beatles had ten thousand hours of practice. Steve Jobs had ten thousand hours, too. You need practice at anything to be able to master it," said Harry. "That's a lot of practice, that's all. I'm still in eighth grade. I have homework."

"Just look at the apps on your cell phone," said Rabbit, pulling Harry's phone from his pocket and punching it with his paw. "You think those apps just happen on their own? Some of them took thousands of hours to perfect. You need time to perfect yourself, Harry Moon. Geesh. Elvis Gold is over twice your age. He is almost thirty, after all. Keep working with me, Harry Moon."

"I know. I will," Harry said. "We did do pretty well at the Scary Talent Show, yeah?" The Scary Talent Show was the Sleepy Hollow Middle School student talent event where Harry had brought down the house when he had used Rabbit on stage in an amazing trick.

"No, we KILLED at the Scary Talent Show. But we just have to keep at it," said Rabbit. "I am here to help and guide and inspire, but you have to be willing to work at it."

"Buddy, I work it pretty hard," said Harry as he gazed out the trees whizzing by the window. He loved the train. It was great fun taking it alone. He felt very grown up.

"I know you do, and so let's keep at it, shall we?"

"We shall, Rabbit, we shall," replied Harry with a smile.

As strong and prepared as we are, sometimes the world still makes us feel small. That is precisely what the world did when Harry got off the Double A train at the Saint John Exit where the AT&T Theatre was located.

There were thousands of people waiting to get into the theater. There were police blockades and police on horseback everywhere. It was a general madhouse. Elvis Gold's followers were true fans, and everyone was more than excited for the opportunity to witness his magic in person.

Because of Elvis' celebrity, the lines to enter the theater were longer than usual. Apparently, there had been a computer malfunction of some sort. The ticket takers had to resort to the manual input of data which simply took longer, so the crowds were pressing in around the doors.

A few weeks back, Harry had sent Elvis Gold a personal letter of appreciation, hoping that he might have a short "hello" with him backstage after the concert. It was a very respectful note. It stated that Harry admired Elvis' stage presence and flair, and he simply wanted to shake his hand and thank him "face to face."

But Harry's heart shriveled to the size of a peach pit when he saw the massive crowds. "There's no way I am going to shake Elvis Gold's hand today," Harry thought to himself.

When he finally got to seat 12D, Harry was quite overwhelmed. He was short for his age, and all the other audience members seemed to tower over him. He looked around and realized he was the youngest one in the crowd. Most of the crowd was young adults or teenagers.

The AT&T Theatre was new and gargantuan. It was a sleek, modern theater in the round. A great rotunda brought the building together in a pointed apex that lurched toward the heavens. On this day, if you looked up, you felt like you were in a great cathedral of magic.

Because of the computer malfunction with the ticketing, the event started late. Harry sat in his seat among the hum of the crowd and tapped his feet. He wondered exactly where Rabbit went at moments like this. He knew he was watching the show, but he had no idea from where.

When the house lights finally dimmed, the audience hushed dramatically. The silence was deafening. The crowd sat in collective silence for what seemed an eternity. Harry could hear the breathing of thousands of people, all eyes darting around in the darkness, looking for their magician hero. Elvis Gold finally appeared above the audience in a silver flash. He was dressed as a ghost in a white captain's uniform sailing over the crowd. The theater gasped and burst into a thunderous ovation. Elvis Gold was here, and he was about to deliver big time!

The light around Great Gold pulsed and became wave-like. The illusion, created by both technology and Elvis's fertile mind, made it appear as if Elvis floated above the crowd at sea. There were flashes of lightning and roars of thunder pumping through the speaker system, adding to the illusion of his stormy entry onto the stage.

Finally, Elvis Gold fell from the invisible ship and was flung across the stage. He hit the wooden floor with a whoosh, sliding on his belly, wearing a captain's cap and uniform. Then, in an amazing feat that left the audience buzzing, a jungle began to grow on stage all around him—palm trees, ferns, and streams of the green world took over the theater. Elvis Gold seemed to have transported everyone in the room to a tropical island. Harry was breathless.

Elvis was clearly lost at sea on this island. A massive wind howled, tearing at Elvis' hat and uniform. The wind tore the clothes from his body piece by piece until Elvis was down to a banana leaf over his private parts.

"Well, that's a bit self-serving," said Harry to Rabbit, who had appeared from somewhere during the opening sequence and was now sitting with Harry in the theater.

"This coming from a guy who stares in the mirror half the day," replied Rabbit.

30   "I am waiting for my beard to start showing," said Harry.

"Sure, sure," said Rabbit.

"Boy, he sure does have the stage presence thing down," said Harry, "I will give him that. Shhh. Watch."

For the next two hours of the show, Elvis Gold became master of his island. He was like a god to the animals. He made elephants vanish. With the mere command of "Abracadabra," a giraffe appeared, and a chimpanzee came with him, riding down the animal's long neck to jump on Elvis and become his friend. The audience reacted with a great "aww," when Elvis and the cute chimp became friends, the chimp riding in the crook of Elvis' arm.

Harry Moon was surprised by how much he loved the show. He studied it carefully like an apprentice studying a master's work. Rabbit leaned over to Harry and whispered something, pointing his paw at the "light detractors." These were built into the act and pulled the audience's attention to focus on one area of the stage while Elvis Gold was getting ready for the next trick on another. It is what is called the "sleight of hand" and how good magicians performed their magic, by getting someone to look at something else so they could do something 'magical' before that someone looked back again.

"Wow, he's really good," Harry whispered to Rabbit.

"There is not a better illusionist in the world," Rabbit replied.

"No one," said Harry as he watched the seeming superman.

"But then you are not an illusionist," said Rabbit. "You have real magic, Mr. Moon."

"But he has better tricks," said Harry.

"BEST ENOUGH"

I n his final performance of the show, having tamed the wild beasts of the island, Elvis stepped into a space pod that arrived on stage. The Great Gold waved goodbye to his jungle and the animals. As the space pod rose into the dark air of the rotunda, the air grew bright with stars. The pod containing its superstar vanished up into the star field.

The crowd leaped to its feet and let out a thunderous ovation. Their Gold had given them an experience they would talk about for years, and they wanted him to know how much they loved it. The applause seemed to go on forever, with people screaming for more. Harry was on his feet as well, screaming for more. He hated that the show was over.

Even though he sensed it was an impossible task, Harry Moon took a deep breath and excused himself down his row and into the aisle, resolved to find his way backstage.

He pushed into the crush of fans clogging the theater and headed toward the exit. Even though he had no idea how he would do it, Harry battled against the crowd toward the stage.

A security guard stopped Harry at a side door. In his gray uniform with yellow piping, he looked down at Harry. The guard seemed like a giant with a massive lantern jaw and dark eyes which slithered over Harry, searching for something.

"Where's your backstage pass?" grunted the guard.

"I don't have one, sir, but I think I might be on a list somewhere. Could you check, please?"

"I don't keep the list. That's held inside, but I can't let you check without a backstage pass."

"I wrote a letter to Mr. Gold. It was a really good letter" said Harry Moon, "I am not bragging. I just put a lot of time in it. I did ten revisions before I sent it on to Mister Gold. I believe in the magic of letters. They can be pretty powerful, don't you think?"

"Yes," said the guard, "sometimes. Depends how they are written."

"So, I am keeping my fingers crossed and hoping I might be on the list." Harry looked up at the giant guard with pleading eyes.

The guard shook his head and smiled. He

was paid to protect Elvis Gold, but he also had a heart. And he was a dad. With a twinkle in his eye, he bent down toward Harry and whispered, "Tell you what, kid. Run quick and see. But if you aren't, promise you'll come right back to me."

"I sure do promise," Harry said. "Thank you."

And just like that, the guard opened the huge industrial door and let Harry slide through. Harry was surprised to see there were a number of fans waiting to see Elvis Gold, all wearing golden backstage passes on their lapels or belts. Harry felt naked since he didn't have one.

When Harry finally reached the thin man in pale shirt and black glasses who held the clipboard, he mustered as much confidence as he had and said clearly, "I believe I may be on your list, sir."

"What is your name?" asked the thin man.

"Harry Moon," Harry replied.

"Spelling like the moon in the sky?" asked the man.

"Yes."

"I see a Yi-Kin-Moon," said the man, his eyes searching for the name as he flipped through pages on his clipboard. "But, unfortunately, no Harry Moon."

Harry's shoulders slumped a bit, and he sighed. He thought his hard work on the letter and his many tries would eventually triumph, but it did not appear that would be the case. This day, he wasn't getting in to see Elvis Gold.

With stooped shoulders, Harry shuffled back through the crowded corridor. He thanked the lantern-jawed security guard for helping him.

"Never stop trying, Harry Moon," said the security guard. "Remember if we don't at least try, we never have a shot at the opportunity."

"I know. Yes, you are right," Harry said to the guard. "Thanks for your help."

"You are welcome," the guard said with a smile. As Harry walked away, he felt the need to say one last thing to the guard.

"And never stop believing, sir," Harry said as he turned back to him. "Never stop."

As Harry moved to the exit through the round stage, Rabbit came alongside Harry, walking with him step by step.

"Hey, at least you took the shot," said Rabbit. "Now you'll just have to wait for him."

"Wait for him? Whaddaya mean?"

"Talent always makes itself know, Harry. He'll find you one day."

"Find me? Why would he want to find me?"

"So he can learn from you."

"Learn from me?"

"About the real magic," said Rabbit.

"Why? He has it all."

"But he doesn't know yet about enough."

"Enough?"

"It's what you have. Enough. You are full of enough, Harry, when you walk with me. When I am helping you and encouraging you, you are finding it's enough. Someone like Elvis Gold is always looking for the next trick. He will want to understand what you are all about. About what fills you and where your magic comes from. Trust me."

"If you are enough, then maybe I can stop practicing?"

"Practicing simply helps you with perfecting your enough. The problem, Harry, is that you are coming into an age of comparison. You stand at the mirror and study your reflection. You think you are not handsome enough or smart enough or fast enough. You compare yourself with everyone else, and you become sad. This is a big problem in middle school.

Everyone does too much comparing. Each of us is on our own path. We have to measure our self against our self and no one else.

"Just become your best enough, that's all I am saying," said Rabbit.

"Okay," said Harry.

Outside, Harry stopped at one of the eight silver *Elvis Gold In the Jungle* souvenir vans. Harry bought a life-size color poster of Elvis as well as his autobiography, *My Golden Life*.

Harry took the train back to Sleepy Hollow. He got off in the town center and stepped into what was left of a sunny Saturday afternoon, walking from the square to his home on Nightingale Lane.

"There you are! How was the show?" asked Honey Moon as Harry came through the front door. "Want an oatmeal cookie? It has raisins. You can pick them out."

"Awesome," replied Harry. "No thanks to the

cookie. Not hungry." He went into his room and closed the door.

That night, he read Elvis Gold's autobiography from cover to cover. Elvis had been a poor kid in the Bronx who discovered magic early when he played Eggshell Monty on the streets to make money for his starving family.

Elvis scrappily worked his way up from there in his hard-knocks life. Following the fashion designer Ralph Lauren's cue, Elvis also changed his last name of "Lipchitz" to "Gold." After all, who would want to buy socks that were named "Ralph Lipchitz" or attend a "Lipchitz" magic show?

Now, Elvis Gold *(Lipchitz)* had mansions in three states and villas in both France and Italy. He had seven race cars peppered throughout the world. He dated starlets and princesses but never committed to them, leaving a trail of broken hearts all around the globe. He had won awards on every continent. Yet, when Harry Moon of

Sleepy Hollow, Massachusetts finished the autobiography, he felt sad for Elvis Gold. He had everything, and yet he had nothing.

He didn't have enough.

He certainly didn't have a Rabbit.

Still, for Harry Moon, it was a struggle to keep himself focused as Rabbit had encouraged him. He practiced his magic just like he should. He worked on his posture. He practiced his presence. He became an expert at all the illusions contained in the golden box of the *Elvis Gold Amazing and Spectacular Magic Set for Ages Eight to Twelve.*

His mom made a deal with Harry that every Tuesday night he could open her book club night with a new magic trick. After all, just like Steve Jobs or the Beatles, he needed to clock his ten thousand hours of practice to be his "best enough."

The book club was composed of a small audience of twelve nurses from his mom's work

at the Sleepy Hollow Hospital. But it was an audience, nonetheless, and they met every Tuesday at 7:00 p.m. sharp to discuss the book of the month. They sat at three different tables in the great room of the Moon house.

To Harry, the women smelled really good and looked really nice. It was like being in a garden in spring time. While the bologna and watercress tiny tea sandwiches were being served, Harry went to work with his magic.

He pulled a pink hanky from Mrs. Kenyon's ear. He read Mrs. Toledo's mind and told her that she was thinking of the Ace of Clubs.

Despite the applause, Harry Moon was not really a happy guy. The living room, on Nightingale Lane, was not exactly the AT&T Theatre in Boston.

Even when he produced Rabbit from the golden bowler hat, it did not seem to create near as much excitement as Elvis had produced on stage.

"I saw Mrs. Peterhans yawning, Mom," said Harry, grumbling into his Cheerios at the breakfast table.

"Oh, Harry. Cut her some slack. That's not because of you. She has those newborn twins at home who aren't sleeping through the night. She was tired, that's all."

"Even if she was tired, Mom, my magic should be good enough to keep her awake!"

Harry probably should have been grateful that his mom gave him the opportunity to practice. Because you need to practice to become good enough for anything. You don't just show up at the finals at the Olympics. You don't just arrive at the Super Bowl.

"I swear, Harry Moon, I cannot compare you and Rabbit to anyone else in the world. For my book club, you are enough for all of us," said his mom.

45

46

THE VOICES

While bringing the fresh-pressed laundry into her son's room one Saturday morning, Mary Moon noticed a life-sized man tacked to Harry's bedroom wall

"Harry, what is Tarzan doing on this newly painted wall?" cried his mom.

"That's not Tarzan, Mom." replied Harry.

"Sure that is, honey. I mean, look at him, he's in a loincloth, he's half naked, and he's hunched over like an animal, grunting. Tarzan was raised by monkeys, you know."

"It's Elvis Gold, and he's summoning the magic, Mom. Don't you see those chains around him? He's busting them with his power."

"Power? You know where the only true power comes from Harry. I'm not looking at it on your wall."

"Mom, you know that, and I know that. Elvis Gold doesn't have REAL power. He is an illusionist. He is an expert at *the sleight of hand*."

"How can he hide his hand? There's nowhere to put it! He is dressed like a caveman in a loin cloth!"

Mary Moon sighed as she put Harry's clean clothes in the pine drawers of his dresser.

"That's the point, Mom. He's so good that he is doing the sleight of hand without *anything* hiding the trick. He is THAT good. He is my hero."

"Hero? Be careful who you pick as heroes, Harry." Mary Moon sighed. "You are so very different. Horace Turner has that darling Mickey Mouse on his wall. Mark Rutherford has Luke Skywalker. But my son? He has Elvis Gold in a loin cloth."

49

Once Mary Moon finished distributing the laundry, she left his room like she often did, shaking her head. Of course, Mary loved Harry and, likewise, Harry loved Mary. Sometimes, they simply were frustrated with one another.

In those days of practice and more practice, the only one that did not seem to frustrate Harry Moon was Elvis Gold.

For one thing, he was a silent poster on the wall and seemed to agree with everything that Harry had to say. Harry Moon liked Elvis Gold's quiet approval. In fact, he liked Elvis

Gold better than Sherlock Holmes, who was a bona fide, gold-standard genius detective in *The Adventures of Sherlock Holmes*.

"Harry, why would you, just *why would you*—hide that knife," asked the imaginary Sherlock, as he circled Harry, sizing him up, "in your back pocket at 5:00 p.m. before retiring to dinner. Isn't that because you were planning to do away with Melissa Mapplethorpe during desert? But, you didn't need to use the hidden knife, did you, Harry, because Count Basil from Detroit beat you to it!"

"Stop it, Sherlock, it's a darn PLASTIC knife."

"You don't think I noticed, while we were talking, while I was circling you, what I really saw, Harry? I saw a weak attempt at the one-arm vanish. Your magic is pathetic! I saw you replace that plastic knife with the dagger you were planning to use on Miss Mapplethorpe! Your sleight of hand cannot hide your wicked, wicked heart from me, Moon!"

Harry had had it. He pulled the plastic

knife from his pants, turned, and waved the dagger through Sherlock Holmes' illusionary wool vest.

"That was not plastic, Harry!" Sherlock said.

"And you're not real, Sherlock," Harry said as he watched ghostly Holmes fall to the floor.

"Sorry," Harry said. "But, you are simply a figment of my imagination so I kinda can do what I want with you."

51

"Oh really," said Sherlock, looking up at Harry. "Is that what we all are? Elvis Gold, me, *Rabbit*?"

"Well, no, Rabbit is not a figment of my imagination. He is as real as the sunshine."

"Oh really?" said Sherlock. "Then why can't anyone see him?"

"They can. You just have to have the eyes to see, Sherlock. People can see him when I am on stage. Sarah Sinclair can see Rabbit sometimes. Baby Harvest sees him all the time."

"Oh?" said Sherlock as he grabbed the carpet with his hands, "and where is Sarah Sinclair now?"

"High school, probably doing homework. But just because she is not with us right now, doesn't mean she isn't *real*, silly!

"Well, maybe she is and maybe she isn't."

52

"Oh, Sherlock, you can be such an annoying fantasy!" said Harry. With a swipe as fast as a finger on a cell phone, he waved his almond wand over Sherlock and cried, "Abracadabra." And as fast as a blink of an eye, Sherlock was gone.

"Sherlock is correct about one thing," said Elvis Gold as he stood stoic and growling on the wall. "You have not perfected the one-arm vanish."

"Posters can't really talk," Harry said.

"I can," Elvis Gold said from his grunting pose.

"You're not really talking. You're just illusion."

"I am not just a poster, Harry. I am watching your every move. As a magician, you stink."

"Stink? That's awfully harsh, Elvis!" With that, Harry waved the wand of almond that he received from Samson Dupree. "Abracadabra, Elvis Gold!" Harry said as he brandished it across the poster. "Stay silent!"

53

Harry looked over at the growling Great Gold. Elvis did not open his mouth one more time.

Harry sat on the edge of the bed and sighed. He was tired of playing. He was exhausted from practice.

"I get discouraged, Rabbit. All these voices; my Mom, Sherlock, Elvis. Sometimes, I don't know what to think or what to do or who to be! How can I ever compete with Elvis Gold?

He has all the tricks!"

"Harry," Rabbit said, "there will always be discouragement. There will always be disappointment. That is why there will always be a time for heroes."

"I am thirteen years old, and I have no idea why I am here!" said Harry.

"Now you're being silly," said Rabbit.

"But why am I being silly?" asked Harry.

"Because you are here to show people that life is magical," said Rabbit, "By your magic, they can sense a glimmer of the beauty behind reality."

"Yes, I believe in love. I do Rabbit, you have shown me that. You gave me the courage to kiss Sarah Sinclair."

"You found that courage yourself, Harry. I only nudged you a bit."

"And now I have to wait to kiss her again," said Harry. "I don't like that."

"Everything in time, Harry. Find your peace. You want to be courageous."

"Courageous?" said Harry. "How can I be courageous in the face of discouragement? I am telling you, Rabbit, and I hate to have to admit it because I sound like a total wimp, but I was pretty devastated when Mrs. Peterhans yawned at Mom's book club."

Rabbit grabbed his lop ears and made them stand straight up. "That's right, now you are getting it. Courage exists in the face of disappointment, in the eyes of fear."

"I don't get it," Harry replied.

"There will always be trouble, Harry. That's why there will always be a time for heroes. Even when the voices tell you not to be, be courageous!"

Harry listened to what Rabbit said. He

always listened even when he didn't agree. For he knew that, in all things, Rabbit was working for the good of those who loved him. In the *Elvis Gold Amazing Magic Manual for Ages Eight to Twelve*, Harry read that one key element to being "King of Table Magic" was to be confident. Even if you were quaking inside, "be confident!" the manual proclaimed.

So Harry Moon stood at his mirror which hung above his chest of drawers and practiced the face of courage even while he was feeling like a wimp.

He looked at his cheek and popped a pimple. He studied his chin to see if there were any whiskers. Not yet, but there was always tomorrow. And then there was high school. "Yes, show confidence," the manual stated. "With a confident expression, your audience can go anywhere with you."

57

"That's the point," Rabbit said, as he sat on the chest of drawers, observing Harry watch himself in the mirror. "One day when you are holding that stage with as much presence as Elvis Gold, you will be doing what you are designed to do."

"What am I supposed to do again?" asked Harry, shaking the discouraging voices from his mind.

"Reveal the real magic, Harry. Elvis Gold has a wonderful connection with the audience. Great confidence. But Great Gold is simply an illusionist, Harry.

"You, my friend, are a magician. And with practice, steady practice, you will show people the magic of life. Why I would not be surprised, Harry Moon, if you were even able to show that to Elvis Gold someday."

"Ha. Fat chance," said Harry Moon.

"Why is it fat if nothing is impossible when you believe?"

"It just doesn't work that way."

Rabbit hopped over to the bed. "No, Harry, my friend. It actually does work that way if you live a magical life. Why I wouldn't be surprised, one day, if Elvis Gold is sitting in your living room eating your mom's delicious oatmeal cookies."

"And just how could that ever happen?" asked Harry. "That's a little too much dreaming, I think."

"Because this happened."

"What happened?"

"This."

"What is this?" asked Harry

"You are about to find out," replied Rabbit.

Harry scowled at Rabbit. "Sometimes," thought Harry, "sometimes Rabbit is just plain freaky."

60

THE ASTRAL ROAD

s Harry opened the door to the Sleepy
Hollow Magic Shoppe in downtown
Sleepy Hollow, a little bell chimed at
the threshold, signaling a customer. To Harry,
this chime was the most wonderful sound in
all the world—like the ring of an ice cream
truck on a hot day or the gong of the

clock tower on Christmas morning. For Harry, the sound was magical. The chime had a different ring for anyone who entered. For the evil mayor of the town, Maximus Caligula Kligore, it sounded like a fire alarm. For Harry's mom, it sounded like water glasses tinkling as they were set on a table for a delicious and savory hot meal.

As soon as he arrived, Harry was always greeted warmly by the proprietor of the shop, Samson Dupree. No matter what he seemed to be fussing with, Samson was never too busy for his friend. Harry really liked the eccentric old magician. Samson wore a purple cloak, a plastic gold crown, and sparkling red slippers.

Harry had no idea how old Samson was, and he really did not care. Samson treated Harry fairly and respectfully. Like an adult. Harry could ask Samson anything. Even stuff about girls. Even stuff about his non-existent whiskers.

Sometimes, Samson answered before Harry even asked the question. Samson was that special. Harry was not sure if Samson was his guardian angel or just a really old guy. He just knew that the bell and its little chime made him feel very special when he visited the magic shop.

In his journey to better understand his own magic, Harry knew Samson was always there for him. He even gave him his very own rabbit to pull out of a hat. On the record, Rabbit was from Sarah Sinclair. But it was all part of Samson's grand scheme. For there was a great and powerful war going on over the future of Sleepy Hollow, Massachusetts. Harry was a big part of it. Even if he did not know it yet.

63

"Are you sure you are ready?" Samson asked.

Harry was surprised by Samson's question although he should not have been surprised at all. Samson already knew why Harry was there.

"Yes," Harry said, looking at the old man. Samson's plastic, gold crown grabbed the sun slanting through the storefront window.

"You do know that what I am about to teach you is not about keeping Mrs. Peterhans awake during your tricks, don't you?"

"Whaddaya mean?" Harry asked.

"Your feeling great over an attentive audience is not what should be motivating you. What should be motivating you is that your audience feels great."

"How do I do that?"

"By giving your audience what they need. Maybe it is laughter. Maybe charm. Perhaps, hope. What does Mrs. Peterhans need?"

"More coffee," Harry said, shrugging his shoulders.

Samson looked at Harry with a stern face. Samson's eyes flexed, becoming even more focused on him. "Come with me," Samson said. The eccentric old man pivoted. His cloak swirled in the turn. He walked past the cash register. There was a cheery curtain of many colors at the back of the shop. The curtains parted by magic. Samson walked through the opening. Harry shook his head at the way the curtains opened and wondered how he did that. He followed Samson.

The room Harry entered was filled with ancient books. Beakers of potions fumed on burners. Busts of old sages stood on shelves. Harry was not sure if they were Greek or Roman. Samson simply called them "his pupils." A world globe hung next to orbs of crystal and rose quartz. There was a workbench in the far corner. A mound of wands was stacked in that corner, having been whittled and dressed.

A terrifying gray and brown falcon rested on a perch. His hood was over his eyes. Harry breathed a sigh of relief. The falcon was asleep. "Don't worry. Gabriel won't bother you. He's not really here."

"Where is he?" Harry asked.

"On the Astral Road. He's battling some ruffians in Cincinnati."

"What's the Astral Road?" asked Harry.

Samson took the globe from its suspension. "You are good at science, right?" asked Samson.

"Pretty good," said Harry.

"What is life made of? I mean to say, what common elements can be found in both falcon and star?"

"That's easy. There are four elements," Harry said.

"Then would you mind telling me what they are?" Samson asked.

As Harry thought, Samson went to the work island in the middle of the back room. He dropped the world globe onto the wood of the island. It bounced up to the ceiling like a beach ball. It fell onto the wood of the island and shattered like glass.

"The world. It is like the falcon or the star. It is all life. The world—you and me—we are all of the same elements. While you name the elements, I will pull them from the world," Samson said.

"Okay," Harry said as he looked at the perfectly good globe now in pieces on the surface of the work island.

"Fire is an element," Harry said. Samson opened his right hand over the shattered globe and wiggled his fingers.

As the old man moved his flat palm over the ruins, flames leaped from the glass. Samson turned his fingers into his palm and made a fist. The flames gathered in a ball of conflagration in midair. Harry stared at the small ball of fire.

"Wow," was all Harry Moon could utter. "THAT's pretty cool. Want to learn that."

"We'll talk later. What is the next element?" Samson asked.

"Water," Harry replied.

Samson opened his fingers and spread his flattened palm over the remains of the globe. Fine droplets of rain lifted from the pieces. Harry watched in amazement as the rain gathered in a second ball, this one of water.

Each time, Harry answered, Samson lifted his hands, and each time the shattered remains grew less on the wooden isle.

"Clay or earth," Harry said. "Air," he replied. And then finally, there was nothing left of the globe. It was now in a new form—four separate and disparate spheres floating in the air.

"Look at all the space between the elements," Samson said quietly. "Put your hand between the gaps of the four elements," he prompted Harry.

Harry stood on a chair and swiped his hand between the ball of fire and the ball of water. With Samson's prodding, Harry swiped his hand over and under the spheres. "Science says that if you collapsed all the space between the elements, the entire universe could fit in a bucket," Samson said. "Imagine Harry, a bucket."

"Then there's a lot of space between matter," Harry said.

"So much so that we magicians call it the Astral Road. That's how the falcon, Gabriel, traveled to Cincinnati. He traveled

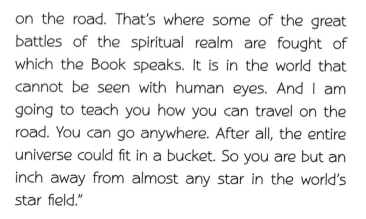

on the road. That's where some of the great battles of the spiritual realm are fought of which the Book speaks. It is in the world that cannot be seen with human eyes. And I am going to teach you how you can travel on the road. You can go anywhere. After all, the entire universe could fit in a bucket. So you are but an inch away from almost any star in the world's star field."

"Samson," Harry said watching the four spheres, "but Gabriel ... look over there. He is still on his perch. How can he be traveling if I can see him still here?"

"Ah," Samson said with a smile in his voice. "Not all of Gabriel is here. Gabriel is traveling with his soul. You see, all this space? Do you know what it is called, Harry?"

"You mean the fifth element? Is that what it is called? I have heard the name before," asked Harry.

"The fifth element is not often recognized by science. That is where we magicians disagree

with science. The fifth element is the unseen—
it is spirit. We travel by our souls through the
spirit that holds all of life together."

Harry watched as Samson arched his
palms and held them in a half circle.

"It is the spirit that holds the four elements
together. That holds all matter in place," Harry
said, thinking out loud.

"And the spirit is alive. It is the source of
all other life. It remains a mystery to science,"
Samson said with a smile.

"But it is not a mystery to we magicians?"
asked Harry.

"Oh, it is still a mystery to many," said
Samson.

He had a smile in his voice as he lifted his
hands. Harry watched as Samson's cupped
hands moved closer to the four spheres floating
in the air. As his hands came closer to the
spheres, they converged. There was the globe

once more. It was as if it had never been shattered.

"So that spirit that holds all of life together is who we know as God?" Harry asked.

"You will have to find the answer to that question, my friend, inside yourself. Look for the answer within."

"But you know," Harry said. "I know you know."

"Each person must find his own way. That is the way that is told to us by the Great Magician. So only through your life, in your way, shall you know what you must know. I can only tell you about the Astral Road. There is not much space between the stars. You wanted new magic. I will point you toward the road, but you will have to find the way. As with much in life, you have to grow small, before you can become great."

In the weeks ahead, Samson Dupree demonstrated to Harry Moon how to become smaller than the elements so that he could travel in the space between things.

Imagine, Harry Moon became even smaller than the colors of the world. They loomed large and formidable; the primary four colors that comprise all color—red, blue, green and yellow. Harry became smaller than even that. Imagine.

It is often said that a tourist goes to a place and sees with his or her eyes.

A traveler goes to a place and sees with his soul.

Harry became a traveler.

In this manner, and through much discipline, Harry learned how to take other souls with him in the journey. One soul even brought a cellphone. She took a video and then everything in the world changed for Harry Moon. But that is getting just a little ahead of our story.

When Harry looked at Samson that day in the Sleepy Hollow Magic Shoppe as Samson hung the world globe back on a string, Harry felt good.

He knew that Samson trusted him.

He knew he would find a way to use this new power for good. And Harry's first use of the power was to discover the solution to Mrs. Peterhans' sleeping problem.

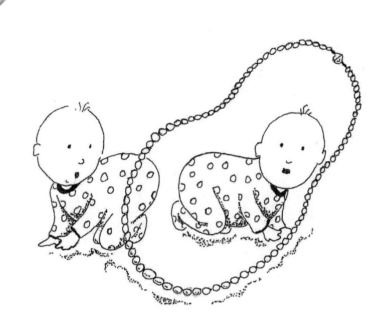

CAUGHT ON TAPE

A t the Tuesday night book club, Harry
Moon was on fire.

Not literally, of course. He had practiced
hard in his bedroom for weeks for this night.
For Harry, this was his Olympic finals. This
was Super Bowl Sunday, even though he was
simply performing for twelve nurses including
his mom in the great room on Nightingale
Lane.

Sure enough, as the chimes of the Moon grandfather's clock rang seven times, Harry Moon, in his amazing gold cape and sparkling gold bowler hat, stood before the three card tables to find Mrs. Peterhans opening her mouth to yawn.

She was quick to stifle the yawn with her hand so that Harry Moon would not see. But to a magician like Harry, Mrs. Peterhans' sleight of hand needed some heavy practice.

"Mrs. Peterhans," said Harry Moon in a gentle voice, "are those twins keeping you up at night?"

"Why do you say that, Harry?" asked Mrs. Peterhans, smiling and a little embarrassed.

She was a nice looking lady with chestnut hair and naturally flush cheeks. She always wore her very nice, saltwater pearl necklace that her husband had bought her on their honeymoon in the Bahamas.

"You seem to be stifling a little yawn there..." said Harry with a smile. He understood her.

"Oh, I am sorry, Harry. But with twins, you know, from midnight to sunrise, it always seems to be feeding time. If it's not one awakening, it's the other. I hope you know, Harry, I look forward to your opening trick every week. I am just a little exhausted tonight, that's all."

"No worries, Mrs. Peterhans. I am here to help. Come on up here, and let's see what we can do."

11

"Do?" she said, looking around the room as she got slowly to her feet. "What on the earth can you do?"

"Come on up here, Mrs. Peterhans! Come on up here and get a dose of some real magic!

"Oh, alright," she said shyly, making her way past the ladies. "I deserve this for yawning. I am so sorry, Harry!"

"Nothing to be sorry about, Mrs. Peterhans! Come on up!" Harry said with a smile. The women in the book club applauded as she walked forward. You would have thought that Mrs. Peterhans was in the Grand Ballroom at Caesars Palace in Las Vegas for all the drama and excitement.

Harry tipped his golden bowler to Mrs. Peterhans as she joined him at the fireplace where he always conducted his show. He was pleased with the clapping. Even though he was nervous, he could sense his strength growing. He was confident in the face of nerves. He was courageous even if he wasn't quite sure where his magic would take him.

"Thank you, Mrs. Peterhans," said Harry. The nurse was extremely tall, making the short-for-his-age Harry seem even more minuscule. But this did not bother Harry Moon. Being short was who he was. Tonight, he was still short but tall in courage. He had practiced as much as he could. Tonight, he was the great magician, Harry Moon. Great Gold had nothing on him.

"Let's see what we can do for you," said Harry, "and those two little love bugs of yours."

"Do? DO?" said Mrs. Peterhans with a smile.

"Anything you can do would be a miracle."

"Only the Holy can give us a miracle, Mrs. Peterhans."

"God knows, I have prayed, Harry!" she said with a laugh. The women all nodded. They all had babies once. They knew that it truly was a miracle if they could sleep uninterrupted until dawn.

"Since this will require a miracle, Mrs. Peterhans, will you help me produce Rabbit?"

"Okay."

"We will need Rabbit. Do you know, him, Mrs. Peterhans?"

"Mrs. Peterhans looked around the room with a smile. "Oh, I have heard talk of him."

"He is the spirit between the stars. He is the space between any two people. We simply need to call him to be with us."

Harry took off his golden bowler. With a graceful swipe, Harry revealed the empty hat to the audience. "See nothing, right? Reach inside, please, Mrs. Peterhans. Is there anything in the hat?"

Mrs. Peterhans reached inside the hat and felt around. She pulled her hand out. "Well, I did feel my Pandora bracelet," she said with a smile. The yawning had stopped, and she was wide awake. She even "played" the audience of women a tad. "But here it is!" she said as she held her right hand up, jangling her bracelet with the many charms.

The book club ladies laughed and smiled.

Harry was pleased. The audience seemed more engaged with him than ever before. Going to Boston to see Elvis Gold live was paying off. Harry's give and take with the audience was better, for sure.

"So, there is nothing in the hat now?" Harry asked as he held the bowler up to Mrs. Peterhans again.

"Not that I could see or feel," she said. "I'm quite sure that it is completely empty."

"Exactly!" said Harry. "But even though you could not see it or feel it, it was still there, Mrs. Peterhans. For often that which is most essential is not seen with human eyes."

Harry grabbed the almond wand that Samson Dupree had given him from the mantel on the fireplace. He held it over his head and made large circles with it like a rodeo cowboy turning his lasso in the air. It wasn't much. But it was enough to get the women's attention. They were mesmerized by Harry's simple, smooth movements. Mrs. Kenyon's mouth dropped for she felt she was watching an acrobat flying from swing to swing in Cirque Du Soleil.

As Harry Moon waved his almond wand over the brim, he leaned over and whispered, "Abracadabra!"

"I meant to ask you, Harry, what does

'Abracadabra' mean?" interrupted Mrs. Peterhans as she pulled at her saltwater pearls a bit apprehensively. "I always wondered about that."

"In a moment, Mrs. Peterhans. First, we are going to get Rabbit to help you with your babies."

Harry placed the wand back on the mantel. With both his hands firmly on the sparkling brim of the golden bowler, he said to Mrs. Peterhans. "If you wouldn't mind, would you please reach inside once more?"

Mrs. Peterhans reached inside the hat with her right hand. She jumped, and her awakened look now turned to surprise.

"Oh my gosh!" she cried as she felt something. "There is something in there. That's impossible."

"You are going to need both hands for this, Mrs. Peterhans. Rabbit is very big."

She nodded. "If you say so, Harry." Mrs. Peterhans' voice had grown tremulous. She took her left hand and placed it into the bowler along with her right. She yanked at the insides of the hat.

"Oh my, I think I have both his ears," she said with excitement. The women in the room were staring at the two in stone silence. No one knew what to expect next.

"Those would be my ears," grunted Rabbit's voice from within the bowler.

"Oh my gosh! Did you hear that?" Mrs. Peterhans said as she turned to the ladies sitting in the room. "The hat talked! Harry made the hat talk!"

They nodded their heads in disbelief.

"Strong but gentle, Magdalene, I am very sensitive," said Rabbit from inside the hat.

"Did you hear that, ladies? The thing knows my name. How are you doing that, Harry Moon!"

"I am not doing a thing, Magdalene. I am Rabbit."

"Oh my gosh, I have the rabbit! I have the rabbit in my hands!" said Mrs. Peterhans as she pulled and pulled and slowly Rabbit was revealed. Out came his beautiful lop ears, one white, one black, and then his harlequin face and his bright dark eyes and then his snow white tummy and his haunches peppered in black and white.

He was an enormous rabbit, and he stood half as tall as Harry Moon when Mrs. Peterhans set him on the floor.

"Wow, wow, wow!" said Mrs. Teboe. She had pulled her iPhone from her purse and was videotaping the trick.

"What the heck?" said a stunned Mrs. Weinstein. "How did he do that? That's the most unbelievable thing I have ever seen. That rabbit is even bigger than the hat! That's impossible!" The women were all talking at once. Mary Moon sat back in her chair and looked at her son with utter amazement.

"So, in answer to your question, Magdalene..." said Rabbit as he turned to look up at the tall nurse.

"My question?" Mrs. Petterhans said in a daze. Her cheeks had gone flush, and she was clearly a bit of a mess. Her right hand was fidgeting with such pressure on her pearls that she broke her necklace. The white saltwater pearls fell from her neck scattering everywhere on the earth-colored carpet. "Are you TALKING?! YOU ARE A RABBIT!"

The women in the room stopped chattering about what they were seeing, and all eyes and ears were on Harry and Rabbit. Harry Moon had produced a talking rabbit. This was magic none of them had ever experienced before.

"Yes, I am. To your question on what does 'Abracadabra' mean? Here, let me get those for you," said Rabbit as he looked down at the many pearls. He turned to Harry with a nod.

Harry picked up his wand and waved it over the carpet.

"Abracadabra," intoned Harry Moon. He was having a hard time not smiling. The reaction of the women to Rabbit was funny.

The women gasped as the white pearls lifted into the air at Harry's command. Like a charmed cobra, the silicon thread around Mrs. Peterhans' neck waved to the pearls suspended in the air. One by one by one, the saltwater gems arrived at the thread. Mrs. Peterhans looked down to check out the little drama happening around her neck. Her eyes grew large as the pearls moved like little cars racing onto the highway that was the thread. The string closed, and the pearl necklace became what it once was. Whole. The entire room of women gasped. They had never seen anything like this before.

"Abracadabra is an ancient command," said Rabbit. "As you may know, 'A' is the beginning of the Greek alphabet. When the command is spoken with a sincere heart, the beginning is

unleashed for good purpose."

"The beginning?" asked Mrs. Peterhans.

"Yes, the beginning has many names. Many believe it is the beginning that sets all of life into motion."

"So, Mrs. Peterhans, are you ready for that help now?" asked Harry Moon.

"I'm sorry, the help? There is more to the trick?" asked Mrs. Peterhans.

"Help to end your exhaustion," replied Harry Moon. "The babies. Rabbit is here to help with the babies. And this isn't a trick at all. It's magic."

"Oh yes, I am!"

Harry smiled as Mrs. Peterhans, and the women looked with eyes of wonder at Harry and Rabbit.

"Get ready, for on the count of three, we are

going to move through space and visit your babies, Noah and Nathan."

"Now? Right now?" said Mrs. Peterhans incredulously. "But how?"

"Yes, now," said Harry Moon.

"Oh, the nursery is a mess," said Mrs. Peterhans, "being a working mom with twins and no help, and of course Paul, my husband, helps as much as he can but..."

89

"Never you mind, Mrs. Peterhans. Don't sweat the small stuff," Harry said, "Rabbit's already gone on ahead of us. He's making things ready for company."

Mrs. Peterhans looked around. Rabbit was gone.

As fast as the command of "Abracadabra," Harry held up the golden cape in front of Mrs. Peterhans.

He was a little short for this particular trip

on the Astral Road, so he stood on an extra folding chair that he pulled from the wall of the fireplace. Harry held his caped arm in front of the tall nurse.

The women at the tables gasped again. For there before them and all around them was the nursery of Noah and Nathan Peterhans.

With the swipe of his golden cape, Harry had transported the book club ladies through the fifth element and onto the second story nursery of a house several miles away. They never knew what hit them. Before them all, there were two pine cribs on either side of the room with a white changing table separating the two cribs. The nursery was papered with fairytale characters. There was Merlin, the magician, Prince Charming, and King Arthur all before the ladies seated in the living room.

Wearing an old-fashioned, poufy blue British nanny cap, Rabbit was doing some last minute folding of laundry at the changing table when the book club arrived in the room.

While Mrs. Peterhans stood, the women clutched their folding chairs as if they were in a rocket ship, fearing they might be ejected with their slightest movement. They had simply traveled through the astral plane, the invisible net behind all of life.

Mrs. Weinstein, leaned into Mrs. Teboe and said, "Are you getting all of this, Debbie?"

"I sure am," said Mrs. Teboe, not taking her eye off the screen of the iPhone, "otherwise who would ever believe us?" It seemed that souls could even take their iPhones through the Astral Road and make videos.

91

"You're not going to run out of tape, are you?" asked Mrs. Weinstein.

"Even though it's called 'tape'...it's not tape anymore. I don't know what it actually is," replied Mrs. Teboe. "All I know, plug it into my laptop, and it plays."

Harry walked over to Noah's crib and peered in. Mrs. Peterhans joined him. She saw that Nathan was sleeping peacefully. She walked past the changing table to the other crib. Little Noah was asleep as well.

Mrs. Peterhans looked at her wristwatch and said as if to herself. "Well, it's only 7:10; it's the hours between midnight and 6:00 a.m. when they keep waking each other up."

"Harry and I have been studying the situation for the last few days when it finally came to us," said Rabbit. "All 'eureka' moments come only after the right and left side of your brain has had time to rest. Then when you least expect it, when you are showering, walking, playing ball, BOOM! inspiration hits. And it's always a doozy! Please, Harry, tell Mrs. Peterhans and our audience about our eureka moment."

Harry looked out at his mom and the ladies who sat in their folding chairs at the far side of the room. He noticed that his mom's mouth was open in shock, and her face had gone pale.

"Here is the secret," said Harry as he looked to Mrs. Peterhans. "Noah and Nathan grew in your womb. They heard your heartbeat, and they felt each other's. It was a super nice time growing inside. Now, there is too much time in the night without those familiar heartbeats. For all of us, it is strange to be here. The mystery of life never leaves us alone. Eventually, they get scared because they have lost the warm familiar of something they have grown to expect. And then they cry. They miss one another's heart too much. At least, they do for now."

93

"What should I do?" asked Mrs. Peterhans.

"Remove the space between them," said Harry.

"Take away the changing table?"

"Take away one of the cribs...at least for a few months," said Harry.

"Sleep in the same crib? Is that a good idea? Won't they toss and turn and hit each other with their hands and wake each other up? Won't it be worse?"

"Trust us," replied Harry. "They will love it for they will feel good to be with the one they have known for so many months in the womb. They are brothers, after all."

Rabbit walked over to Mrs. Peterhans and nudged her at her waist with his paw, "You can do it now, Magdalene."

Mrs. Peterhans reached down into the crib and picked up baby Nathan. She held him close as she walked across the nursery and gently placed him next to Noah.

Rabbit looked into the crib. There were Nathan and Noah sleeping soundly next to one another. Noah turned to his side and propped his tiny legs on top of his brother's back as they snuggled into one another. Rabbit put his paw into Mrs. Peterhans' hand and squeezed. Mrs. Peterhans finally looked at the nanny with rabbit ears and smiled.

"When you get home tonight," said Nanny Rabbit "have a feeding before you go to bed and then place them together. They may not completely sleep until sunrise, but in a few days, you, Paul, and the boys will sleep through the night. By the weekend, you will all be healthier and happier because of this."

Mrs. Peterhans stepped back and looked down at Rabbit.

"Who ARE you?" she said.

"Tell Magdalene who I am, Harry Moon,"

"Rabbit is the space between the stars." Indeed, Harry Moon had listened very carefully to Samson Dupree. Rabbit was the fifth element. Rabbit was spirit.

In a little while, Harry, Rabbit, and the book club traveled back across the astral plane. They returned to the Great Room on Nightingale Lane.

In his golden bowler and his golden cape,

Harry Moon took a bow to great applause as the women all stood and clapped. The women, including Mrs. Peterhans, tried to concentrate on their latest book, but no one could ignore what they had seen. Somehow in the modest three-bedroom Moon house, they had encountered real magic.

"I am confused," said Harry Moon to Rabbit, once there were only the two of them in Harry's room. "Why didn't you call 'Abracadabra' for what it is?"

"What is that?" asked Rabbit as he sat on the bed, reading the thick book, *Beyond Quantum Physics*. He was chortling to himself, "Oh, this is rich!"

"Abracadabra is not a command," said Harry. "It's more of a prayer."

"It's both, really. Anyways, I don't want to get too religious."

"Don't get religious?" said Harry as he tried to concentrate on his American Revolution essay. "But you know it is true!"

"Honestly, Harry, I want people to love each other. Just like Nathan and Noah love one other. In the end, all of us are family. You may and will have enemies, but you must do everything you can to love them, too."

"Rabbit!" said Harry. "Why are you laughing at that physics book? It's smart people trying to figure out the mystery of life!"

"I am not laughing at them, Harry! I am delighted with the progress made by people. They are getting a lot of it right, and so much is still wrong! I am laughing with delight."

Harry went back to his essay and tried to concentrate over Rabbit's giggling. Harry Moon was happy with the show that night. He had practiced hard, and he and Rabbit were now more like an act. It wasn't like the Scary Talent Show with Rabbit grandstanding by flying around the stage. Harry had held his own. There was a good deal of back and forth, making the patter work between Harry and the audience.

When Mrs. Teboe returned home, her daughter, Muriel was still up. Muriel was eight. She was precocious as well as mischievous. A dangerous combination.

"Muriel, can you look at something for your mother?"

"Sure, mom," Muriel said, "what is it?"

"You tell me what you see," said Mrs. Teboe as she sat down at the desk in the family office. She plugged her iPhone into the desktop Mac and let the recording play on the desktop. The screen was a good size so nothing could be missed.

"Are you traveling through space?!" cried little Muriel. Muriel's proclamation brought the rest of the Teboe family into the first story home office. In came Mr. Teboe in his robe and slippers. Next was Mindy Teboe and Max Teboe and Tommy Teboe.

"What are we watching?" asked Mr. Teboe

They could not believe their eyes. When Mrs. Peterhans put the baby Nathan in the crib next to baby Noah, the image went black.

"I guess I lost my battery right there," said Mrs. Teboe.

"What happened next?" asked Mr. Teboe.

"Harry Moon said that they should sleep peacefully for they knew each other even before they were born since they grew alongside each other as brothers."

"What the heck did I just watch?" asked Muriel.

"I think, Muriel," said Mrs. Teboe carefully and gently. "I think...you just watched a miracle."

"A miracle?" asked Mr. Teboe.

"A miracle with a rabbit wearing a nanny's

cap? Who was that rabbit?" asked Muriel.

"I believe so," said Mrs. Teboe carefully and deliberately. "Hey, do you want to know about 'Abracadabra'?" Mrs. Teboe asked her family. No one knew so she explained the mystery behind the command.

That same night, Mrs. Peterhans arrived home and woke her two babies up with their second feeding. This was around 11:00 p.m. She placed the twins next to each other, sang a lullaby, and soon they were asleep. And for the first time in over a month, both Paul and Magdalene Peterhans slept through the night and were awakened by the sunrise.

Muriel Teboe woke up to the sun peeking through her window. In her Princess Elsa pajamas, eight-year-old Muriel ran down the upstairs corridor to the family office. She clicked on YouTube to see how many hits the Book Club Magic Show had gotten. Even little Muriel was surprised.

Magic Show had one million, two hundred thousand and fifty-two hits. It was later said that the comment section alone could wrap around the world five times.

By lunchtime, every possible news channel had surrounded the Sleepy Hollow Middle School.

"Dude," said Bailey Wheeler, as he leaned into his friend, Harry Moon. "This is what you call famous."

Harry, holding his lunch bag, looked out at the cafeteria window and saw the news teams at the floor to ceiling cafeteria window. Looking like a massive tech spider with legs made of cable, the worldwide press was pressing against the glass, trying to capture anything they could of Harry Moon.

Cameras were snapping. Cameras were rolling. Some journalists were calling Harry Moon, 'Young Solomon.' Others called him, 'The Second Coming.' The Boston SWAT Team had arrived with helmets and crowd shields to

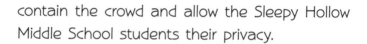

contain the crowd and allow the Sleepy Hollow Middle School students their privacy.

"Harry," said Declan Dickinson, as he sat next to Harry at the cafeteria table. "You can have any girl you want. I bet even Sarah Sinclair is ready to cross the Line of Demarcation just to date you."

"Fat chance, Declan," said Harry.

"I envy you, bro," Declan said. "That magic of yours is a total chick magnet. Just look around."

Harry looked around the cafeteria. Not only were the eyes of the media on him, but so were every person's at every table in the cafeteria. That included a lot of girls. They had all seen the YouTube video.

After Harry finished his ham and swiss sandwich, his apple, and his walnuts, Miss Pryor, the drama teacher and the director of the annual Scary Talent Show, entered the cafeteria. She walked over to Harry and whispered into his ear. Harry rose from the table and walked with Miss Pryor to the principal's office.

"Big doings," whispered Bailey to Declan as Harry was escorted out of the cafeteria.

When Harry Moon walked into the principal, Mrs. Knapp's, office, it was not the first time. He liked Mrs. Knapp who always wore a neatly tailored suit that fit snugly around her ample figure. Harry sensed the principal had his back, even though she often found his brain confounding.

103

In the room were also Mary and John Moon, who had been called in for the caucus. "Well, we seem to have ourselves a little situation here," said Principal Knapp. After much discussion, the adults in the room arrived at the conclusion that it would be best if Harry made a brief statement to keep the press from turning the school into a circus.

"Okay," said Harry as he sat in a chair, looking up at Principal Knapp, "but I would like to talk this over with Rabbit."

"Rabbit? Um, of course," said Mrs. Knapp.

At 1:00 p.m., right after the second lunch bell rang, Harry walked out of the glass door at the front of the school. He passed the SWAT Team who guarded the front and back doors of the school with their shields and helmets. The school was surrounded by a sea of press. That ocean roared with questions and groaned with snapping and rolling cameras.

Harry Moon strode to the podium which stood at the end of the school sidewalk. Miss Pryor walked over and stood next to him to give Harry moral support. In truth, Harry was neither frightened nor disoriented. But he liked Miss Pryor. She had been kind to him. He enjoyed her company.

Miss Pryor took the podium first. She barked like a drill instructor. "Unless you get quiet, people, nothing is going to happen here!"

Harry smiled. He had heard those words from Miss Pryor before. Eighth graders could be pretty rowdy. She always addressed the school assemblies, the talent shows, and the rehearsals with 'people.'

"Zip it now, people!" she said to the crowd.

Miss Pryor explained that there would be no "Q and A." With that, the crowd moaned with disappointment. Miss Pryor further explained that Harry had a prepared statement. As the roar of the crowd finally died down, the questions still came. "Harry, how do you do it? Where does your magic come from? Mister Moon, are you the second coming? What planet is Rabbit from? Where did Rabbit get the name?"

"People, Harry Moon will not say a word unless I can hear a pin drop."

The din of the press quieted while Miss Pryor stared down the crowd. When complete silence came, the only noise was the clicking of the cicadas in the trees.

"A pin drop, people!" She held out her

hand, holding a tiny pin which slipped to the floor. Mrs. Pryor watched it fall and bounce several times as it settled on the ground. She turned to her side to see Harry smiling at her. It was her signature move. She looked back at the crowd.

"People, not a word," she warned. "Here is Harry Moon."

Harry stood on the apple crate that rested behind the podium. He looked out at the sea of mikes and cameras.

"I am just a kid who has Rabbit," Harry said. And it was all that he said.

THE MAN IN THE BOWLER HAT

Talent is a funny thing. It is the great leveler. The gift wraps itself around both the rich and the poor. It springs from both sexes. It arrives at the temple of every human being who has skin, whether black, white, red, olive, brown, or any gradation in between.

One of the wonders of life is that talent always seems to rise. It is hard to put a bright gift under a basket. The light pokes through the spaces in the weave. Like any lit candle, it cannot hide in the dark. The bearer of talent, when met with discipline and hard work, is sure to find a place in the world. Talent simply needs to be cultivated by eyes that can see and ears that can hear. It simply requires a teacher.

This was certainly the case of Helen Keller, a girl some never suspected of having a talent at all.

Helen became blind and deaf as a tiny baby. Imagine living in a world that was dark and silent. The amazing thing about Helen was that she could see things people with eyes could not. With her touch, Helen Keller could see the hearts of people by the mere touch of their face to her hands. People came from all over the world to be seen by Helen as she ran her fingers over their faces. By not having certain gifts, she rose to the light. Her lack of gifts was the gift. Everyone, even someone like Helen, is blessed with gifts.

Harry Moon had a supernatural gift. By his command, objects appeared and disappeared. By his thought, locks on chains would fall away. By his magic, he was unbound.

But what was this certain gift Harry Moon possessed? Making rabbits appear in thin air? Flying to children's nurseries in the middle of the night? How could such a gift be understood? Indeed, Harry Moon's magic could not even be defined by the conventions of the great illusionists.

Throughout history, men and women, boys and girls with unusual talent are almost always sought out, not by the masses, but by those with similar talents. The mentors and sages of renown can encourage, compete, or destroy those with gifts who come behind them.

On this spring mid-afternoon following the press explosion over Harry Moon in Sleepy Hollow, a silver Hercules, a mach-20 commercial helicopter, landed in Melville Field off of Witch Broom Road. Dressed in a silver flight suit, the pilot exited the craft to make certain all was appropriate for the passenger. A black town car waited off the runway for its passenger, a man in a bowler hat. He followed the pilot down the steps of the copter and climbed into the black car. Elvis Gold had come neither to encourage nor to destroy. He had come to understand the unusual magic of one Harry Moon.

Harry Moon was in his bedroom concentrating on his history homework when the knock came at the door. Elvis Gold had arrived at the Moon home on Nightingale Lane. Working over his screen at his desk from his bedroom, Harry Moon shivered. He could feel the presence of Gold's soul.

"I am Elvis Gold," said the man in black to Honey Moon when she opened the door. He took off his signature bowler hat, now in black, when he spoke to Honey. He wore his amulet of purple and gold, an alexandrite. It sparkled in the afternoon sun.

"I know who you are," said Honey Moon, her hair in pigtails. "I've seen you in my brother's room." She was holding Harvest Moon in her arms. Harvest had slathered raspberry Go-Gurt all over his mouth, and Honey was just about to clean her baby brother up.

"We have been expecting you," said Honey Moon

"Oh?" Elvis Gold replied in a fluster of nerves and confusion. "Why is that? I only decided a few hours ago to come up from New York City. Who told you?"

"Harry told me."

Elvis' large eyes squeezed into small slits as he contemplated what she had said. With a furrowed brow beneath the bowler, he scowled and said, "That's impossible. I have never talked to your brother."

"Well, Mr. Gold, he has talked to you. Please come on in and meet him. He is, well... *different*. You'll see."

Honey opened the door wide for the Great Gold. He wore a long, black cashmere coat and in his hand was a large black leather bag. He looked more like a funeral director than a pop superstar. Only a black cashmere scarf flung dashingly around his shoulders suggested his showbiz flair.

"Honey," shouted Mary Moon, "who's at the door?"

112

"Elvis Gold, Mom," replied Honey Moon. "He says he is here to see Harry."

It had been a month since the *Magic Show* YouTube video had gone viral. Even though there were now over five hundred million views of the clip uploaded by eight-year-old Muriel Teboe, the crowds of journalists and gawkers had died down. The SWAT teams who once surrounded the Moon home to protect the Moon Family had gone home. The media went on to other breaking stories, and the family returned to answering their own door.

Mary Moon, wiping her hands on her kitchen

apron, entered the foyer where Honey and Elvis Gold stood.

"Is that really you, Mister Gold?" said Mary Moon with a grin. "Harry said you might be coming by."

"It is," Elvis Gold said, taking off his bowler. "I don't usually make such visits to the home of children, but I have made an exception in this case. I understand Harry is a fan, although I don't understand why he would be expecting me. I just decided to make the visit a little while ago."

113

"Well, we have been expecting you. My son saw you would be visiting, so I have some oatmeal cookies baking in the oven."

"You have cookies baking? I really don't get this."

"Yes," said Mary, "well, it won't be the first thing that will confuse you, believe me." Mary Moon smiled as she ran her eyes over the man in black. "I hardly recognized you with your clothes on," Mary said as she took the illusionist's hand and shook it.

"You've seen the jungle show?" he asked.

"I have seen the poster," Mary Moon replied.

"You look good almost naked," said Honey Moon, as she batted her little lashes at Elvis Gold.

114

"Why don't you take Mister Gold into the living room, Honey?" suggested Mary Moon, "while I get the cookies and some refreshment. Coffee, tea, or soda, Mister Gold?"

"Tea, please," he replied.

While Honey walked Elvis Gold into the living room and presented a seat for him on the new couch, Harvest Moon tried to hand Mister Gold the last half of his strawberry Go-Gurt.

Upstairs, Harry sensed Elvis's soul beneath

his feet. Elvis was making his way to Harry's living room. It now seemed like years ago, instead of weeks, that Harry Moon attempted to go backstage at the AT&T Theatre to shake the hand of Great Gold. The crowds had been overwhelming.

Now, the celebrated illusionist was in the Moon house, just downstairs. Harry shook his head in disbelief. "This is hard to believe, Rabbit," he said quietly. He counted his blessings in wonder. "I do indeed live a magical life," recounting the words of his eccentric magic store mentor, Samson Dupree.

Mary Moon steeped mint tea and pulled the baking tray of oatmeal cookies from the oven as Harry Moon walked down the stairs. Harry ambled across the foyer and toward the living room.

There, on his mom and dad's sofa, sat Great Gold. As Harry entered the room, Elvis Gold stood. To Harry, Elvis was a towering figure in his black suit and black shirt.

"It is a pleasure to meet you, Mister Gold," said Harry as he walked across the carpet to his hero. "I am a great admirer of your work."

Like the growing gentleman that he was, Harry Moon held out his hand for Elvis Gold. Gold took a minute to size up the Sleepy Hollow magician. He was so much younger and smaller than he had imagined. He knew immediately he had wasted his time coming to this house. This was a kid with a few hot tricks. He wasn't a magician at all.

The two of them gave each other a hearty handshake.

"Yes," Rabbit chimed in as he plopped on the coffee table and stared at Elvis Gold, "I have to give you credit. You have marvelous stage presence. Oh yes, and you have a wonderful way of speaking that puts the audience in the palm of your hand."

"Do you hear that, Mr. Gold?" asked Harry.

"Hear what?"

"Oh. I see," said Harry. It told him a little something about Elvis Gold's soul if he could not hear the invisible rabbit.

"See what?" said Elvis Gold nervously. His eyes darted about the room, not sure what he should be seeing. He looked over at the young Harry Moon who appeared to be listening to a voice Elvis Gold could not discern.

"You can't see or hear him yet?"

117

"See who?"

"Rabbit."

"No, I see nothing," replied Elvis Gold. "Should I?"

"If I put him into a trick, then you will see him."

"See who?"

"The Harlequin rabbit.'

"Ahh," said Elvis Gold, rubbing his hands together with anticipation. "Is this the one from the *Magic Show* video?"

"Yes. He does not have a standard name. He is a rare breed, but I find 'Harlequin' too long and cumbersome so that's why I simply call him 'Rabbit.'"

"Rabbit?"

118   "Yes, let me bring Rabbit out for you to see," said Harry.

Honey and Harvest made their exit from the room like they always did when Harry got down to business.

Harry scoured the room for some sort of prop. Rabbit would need to be revealed in a trick for Elvis Gold to see him. He spotted the umbrella stand in the entry foyer. "This will do perfectly!" Harry said in a lilt of delight, overturning the stand, spilling the walking sticks and bright umbrellas onto the marble floor.

As Mary Moon came in with cookies and tea, Harry brought the umbrella stand over to Gold to inspect it. As its barrel on the stand was deep, Gold took the umbrella stand in both hands, examining it. He put his entire arm inside and swirled it around and shook the thing, but he could not find any deception built into the piece. It wasn't a magic trick prop. It was simply a piece of furniture that held umbrellas.

"It appears to hold no lie," said Elvis Gold with an imperious tone.

As Harry Moon nodded to Gold, Harry took the umbrella stand from his hands and planted the stand onto the oak-plank floor of the little living room.

"Kind sir, may I present to you from this empty umbrella stand one of the most beautiful lagomorphs that have ever hopped the meadows of this world."

"Oh, what a lovely compliment," whispered Rabbit from the depths of the umbrella stand.

"Thank you, friend."

From his comfy seat on the sofa, Elvis Gold watched intently as the thirteen-year-old Harry Moon reached into the stand.

"By the command of all that is magical, I say 'Abracadabra!'"

Elvis Gold stared. His eyes darted about, looking for the sleight of hand in the illusion as Harry Moon pulled the heavy hare from the fixture. Rabbit sneezed from the dust inside the umbrella stand as Harry lifted him by the scruff of his harlequin neck.

Harry Moon held the rabbit before him. He was big and luscious and beautiful. His black and white face carried a royal countenance.

121

"Now do you see him, Mister Gold?"

Gold sat back slowly against the sofa, his fingers tapping against his chin. How in the world did the kid do that? It was one of the simplest and seamless tricks he had ever seen. Where did that rabbit come from?

"Um, yes I do. Nice trick. You'll have to teach me that."

"When I put such otherworldly matter

into the frame of a trick, you then are able to glimpse him. The fact is, Rabbit has been here all along. When I entered the room, he was already with me, but you could not see him."

"I hear what you are saying," replied Elvis Gold, "but what are you *meaning?*"

Harry looked at his idol. He was ready to throw down the gauntlet. Harry breathed deeply and said, "You would be an even better magician, Mister Gold, if you only believed."

"Believed in what?"

"In the idea that magic need not be an illusion; that magic is real."

"It is not real," said Elvis Gold, shaking his head. "Magic isn't real. You and I know there is actually no such thing as real magic. It's a craft, a business. I'm the best in the world at my business. Not sure exactly what you are all about."

"I am here before you, Mister Gold, with the proof that there is a deeper magic."

"Deeper magic than mine? I hardly think so," chuckled Gold. "You may be a clever kid, Harry Moon, but it won't get you far in this business. Somehow, you are deceiving me, and I'll have that figured out in a few minutes and get out of your way."

"If that is what you choose to believe," replied Harry, "feel free."

123

"I will try you on my terms," said Elvis Gold, his eyebrows rising in the expression of wager that all men know. Elvis Gold no longer saw a boy before him. He saw his youthful competition. Elvis Gold had come to learn from Harry Moon, but now Elvis' pride was becoming an obstacle to his own growth. He saw Harry Moon as a threat, not as a new, young friend.

"Tsk, Tsk," sighed Rabbit when he saw the blood in Elvis Gold's face rise, "you must calm down, Mister Gold. This boy is here to help you. It does not matter who arrived at whose door. You were meant to meet as brothers, not as enemies."

Elvis Gold, however, could not hear Rabbit. He asked Harry Moon, "So, under my terms, will you humor me with the chains that I have brought?"

"What chains do you have for me?"

Elvis Gold picked up his black Bottega Veneta bag at his feet. The bag was new for the leather shined with fresh tannery polish. The brass hinges were shiny. Gold placed the bag in his lap with the flair of a royal. By such silent countenance, Elvis Gold was making his place known to the boy from Sleepy Hollow. Elvis Gold was successful. He performed so often for kings and queens from Abu Dhabi to England that their royalty had become *his* royalty.

"Steel chains with many locks," replied Elvis Gold.

"Locks for illusions?"

"*Real* locks. Made by the greatest locksmiths of the world. No one, no one could possibly open such fastenings. I assure you they have not been made for my deceptions, but to learn of your truth, for surely," he laughed, "if you could break free of them, I would bow at your golden feet."

"My feet, kind sir, are made of clay. The real magic comes, not from me, but from the Great Magician."

"Then, bring your real magic to the unraveling of these locks," said Elvis Gold, as he shook the leather bag, clanking with chains from within.

"I do not bring the real magic anywhere, Mister Gold," said Harry. "The real magic is already here."

Harry Moon looked about the room. Such a confident glance frightened Elvis Gold, but he did not allow his fear to show upon his waging face. Elvis Gold retained an inscrutable expression.

"Well, Moon, I also have the newest combination locks made by Masterlock of Detroit. The four number combination is so complex that it takes even the supercomputer Watson four hours to determine the combination." Elvis pulled the silver chains from the bag. He held up the thick, four cylinder locks that were opened and hung from the chains.

"Not even you know the combinations, Mister Gold?"

"No," Elvis Gold said, somewhat shaken. "How do you know that I don't know?"

"I went into your mind," said Harry.

Elvis Gold laughed uncomfortably. "Yes? Well, let's not be doing that. I don't know you well enough." Gold coughed. "You will need to read such numbers from the factory in Detroit. Surely that should not be a challenge for your deep magic."

"You make a mockery of my world, Mister

Gold," Harry said, looking into Elvis Gold's soul. "I assure you, the real magic is as real as your hardened heart."

"My hardened heart, Harry? How can you say such a thing? I know many women, and I have a soft heart for each of them."

"Your heart stands as impenetrable as the stone heart of Pharaoh. Even when frogs rained from the sky and the fresh waters of the city turned to blood, Pharaoh would not believe in the magic of the rod."

127

"You speak like the prophet of fairytales."

"Real magic will break your fancy chains, but you still will not believe."

"Oh? So now you see my future as well?"

"I can see your pride, Mister Gold." Harry looked up, past the ceiling as he continued. "It fills the sky. Let me assure you. My magic is as real as the sun that pulls the lily up from the field."

"You are an impressive poet, Moon. But you have yet to impress me with your real magic."

Harry Moon had had enough. He saw that his banter with the great Goliath was only fueling Gold's hardness. Harry Moon knew that he could perform much magic. He also understood the heart of a man or woman could only be melted by the willingness of that man or that woman. Only by such willingness could the real magic inspire the strength of compassion.

"Bring on your shackles, kind sir," said Harry Moon, "and let me, before your eyes, give you a sight that will haunt you for the rest of your days."

With relish in his eyes, the Great Gold stood, the steel chains clanking in his hands. He began to wrap the chains with their padlocks and combination locks around Harry Moon. As he did, Elvis Gold came to the boy-man. He could smell his youth. He sensed the strength of his adversary's shoulders, but it was not a strength he knew. This potency was young and

undisciplined like a colt.

"I will cover you in links, my friend," warned Gold.

"Bury me in them," Harry Moon replied.

130

SHOWDOWN ON NIGHTINGALE LANE

As Mary Moon walked through the entranceway, she spotted the walking sticks and umbrellas on the floor. With a sigh, she picked them up while she looked into the living room. There was her son, covered head to toe with chains. His wrists were hand-cuffed behind his back. His feet were bound together in an iron manacle.

As the mother of a budding magician, Mary had seen a lot of Harry's crazy tricks: sawing Sarah Sinclair in two, levitating P.J. MacLaren in his radio flyer wagon, and turning the feathers from an old basement pillow into honeybees. The chains were a first.

She peeked her head into the room. "Getting to know each other, then?" Mary Moon asked.

"Very well," replied Harry Moon.

Mary started into the living room, carrying the sticks and fallen umbrellas in her arms. She was planning to get that umbrella stand back into the entrance hall where it belonged. When she saw the intensity in their two faces, however, she thought the better of it. Instead, she retreated to the entrance hall. There she propped up the sticks and umbrellas in the corner. "This," she thought, "would be for another day."

Elvis Gold stepped back from Harry Moon. With a nod, he signaled to Harry that his tied and bound work was done.

Like a prayer whispered over a cradle, Harry Moon breathed out with "Abracadabra."

The summoning hush was sung in such a way that the meaning behind the word fell like fresh rain over the links, locks, and numbered tumblers of Harry's imprisoning cocoon. Harry Moon's eyes flashed with lightning at Elvis Gold.

133

Harry Moon's whispers were more than a dare to Elvis Gold. They were Harry Moon's prayer to enter the planes of the unseen. But Elvis Gold greeted Harry Moon's incantation with a sneer, even though, in the marrow of his bones, Elvis Gold knew he was dealing with a towering power. This recognition tore at Gold's pride.

The golden afternoon sun that had once

slanted through the window of the living room turned gray. The room grew so dark that Gold reached out to a table lamp to flick on its light to discern the illusion in Harry Moon's trickery. But the table lamp would not abide. As Gold's fingers turned the tiny knob on the lamp, the electrical wires within shorted. The gas inside the bulb expanded, breaking the glass, tearing apart the filament, sending shards of glass into Gold's hand, entering his skin and flesh. Gold grabbed his hand and screamed.

In the gray light of the afternoon sun, Elvis Gold saw the flesh of his white hand grow red with blood. As the light in the room turned inky, Gold observed his hand becoming black in the growing darkness. He was overcome by the sequence of colors that passed before him, colors of white, red, and black, the color palette of the ancient art of alchemy. The age-old craft had alluded sorcerers, wizards, and magicians since the scribe of Egypt wrote the early code at the base of the Giza pyramids.

Elvis Gold could feel his insides. The chilling marrow of his bones lost all temperature as if the life within him was being drained from his body. A dreaded cold was making his teeth chatter and his knees knock, and the breath streaming from his nose and mouth vanished. He could feel his heartbeat slow down.

The Great Gold stood by only the strength of what we know as soul and looked out into the dark of the living room of the Moon home. He had entered a place where there was no time, perhaps there was not even matter, just a cosmic presence that struck him with a peace and wonder, that, well, he had never experienced before.

135

"Harry Moon, what have you done?" came the voice of Mary Moon from the foyer as she passed into the kitchen. "You have broken every light bulb in this house, young man. As soon as you have finished with your guest, you are marching down to Sears, and you are going to buy this household a baker's dozen of GE bulbs."

"Yes, Mom," yelled out Harry with a sigh.

The darkness in the living room was complete. Elvis Gold could not sense his toes, his legs, his hands, or his face. Yet he knew that what was happening had not fully happened yet. In the unseen world, Gold's consciousness remained aware. As he could not move his mouth and form words, he formed his thoughts with his mind.

Why have you not allowed me to see your illusion? Elvis Gold's mind asked.

My magic is transparent, Mister Gold. The choice to see is yours, not mine, Harry Moon replied.

In the dark, Gold heard clattering all around him.

What is that? Gold's mind asked.

It is the chains falling off.

How can that be?

It has taken me longer than I thought.

The numbers to the combination locks were buried behind many walls of safes and concrete in the Masterlock office in Detroit. It took a little doing, but I was able to get the numbers inside the innermost safe.

The dark living room swelled with a silvery mist, which pushed up from the floor-boards. With his consciousness floating, Elvis Gold could see the knots rising through the pine floor as the mist rose. Such a reveal brought a suspicion to Elvis Gold's perception. His pride returned, and he suddenly knew in his mind the truth behind Harry Moon's trickery.

137

As the silvery mist expanded, the room took on the density of the metal. While Elvis Gold could not move his body, he was overwhelmed with the weight of the silver light. But even in the thickness of it, it sparkled.

What is this? Gold's consciousness asked.

Transmutation. Harry Moon replied.

You know such a secret?

Not the secret itself, but I have access to the real magic that knows such secrets. For you see alchemy is not three steps but four. And there are not four elements to this world, Mister Gold, there are five.

As Elvis Gold's consciousness watched, the silver light dimmed and fell away from view. Returning to the room was the slanted golden light of the afternoon sun shining through the open window.

138

Through the wooden window frame came the sound of children at play, kicking a can down the street. There was the sound of nightingales, entreating the twilight to arrive.

Elvis Gold watched as Harry Moon straightened up on the paneled pine floor, free of the manacles, shackles, and handcuffs of his imprisonment. Harry Moon stepped up and out of the pile of chains that were at his feet. He had broken free from that which Gold said was impossible to break.

"I know the illusion, and it is as old as

sorcery itself," Gold said. He realized he no longer was talking by his thoughts alone. His mouth was moving. He looked down and saw his shoes. He looked to his hand. What once was red with blood had now returned to an unblemished white.

"Even when you see the miracle of transmutation, you choose to see illusion," replied Harry Moon. He took a book from the side table and with its edge, brushed the glass of the broken light bulb into the center of the table.

139

"The trick is in the floor boards. I saw it when the silver light drifted up from the knots in the floorboards. Do you mind?"

"Please, Mister Gold, investigate it all. Our home is yours to roam."

Gold walked to the center of the room. While dressed formally in a dark suit, the illusionist went to his knees and crawled across the pine boards. With agile hands, he placed his fingers into the gaps, and poked at

the dark knots of wood, looking for hinges or vulnerability in the floorboard.

"Well, Moon, you are certainly skillful, I will give you that," Gold said as he yanked on the floorboards.

"Skillful?"

"Your trapdoor is indecipherable from this vantage point. You have made darkness your friend. In the black cloak, the sleight of hand is easily hidden. However, I will say that when you manufactured the blackout, it was extremely dramatic. I do understand, Moon, that as an illusionist, you can not divulge your secrets, and that I may never figure out the cleverness of your trick."

"Sorry to disappoint you, Mister Gold. No trapdoor, no trick. I am not an illusionist like you, Mister Gold. I am a magician," said Harry Moon, "So I am happy to reveal what I know, for in doing such, it would be my hope that you might grow up a little."

141

142

THE BASEMENT

"You have no problem showing me what lies beneath these boards?" asked Elvis Gold with a mischievous smile.

"Please, you are my guest here," replied Harry Moon.

"Then lead the way, Harry."

"I shall take you to the basement. But

please know, Mister Gold, I do not consider ALL darkness my friend. Yes, I do like the night. The moon and the stars would not shine without an evening sky. I shall hope one day to hold the hand of the girl I love under the stars which brighten the night. The stars, they can only shine if there is darkness.

"But there is a different darkness that is not my friend. Did you not hear it screaming as the light changed in the room? Did you not hear the hissing of the snakes and screeching of the dragons? They were beneath my heel, Mister Gold, dying under the hammering power of the real magic. No, not all darkness is my friend. I find some of it to be my enemy, and it is the one thing that is unredeemable."

"OK, OK. Will you take me to your basement now?" asked Elvis Gold. "I am anxious to see."

"Indeed, and I will turn on every light I can find so you can inspect my backstage with all your senses."

Harry Moon led the way through the door beneath the first-floor stairwell. Together, with Elvis Gold following, they walked down the wooden steps.

Holding true to his word, Harry Moon flicked and switched every light that he could find at the electrical panel next to the furnace. Harry Moon even found a stepladder so that Gold could climb it and examine the floorboards from the other side.

Elvis Gold ran his eyes and finger across every surface of the basement. The investigation took a good two hours.

"Well, you are really good. Exceptionally skillful. I cannot find the deception," Elvis Gold finally announced. "Well done."

"No deception," Harry Moon smiled faintly.

"Whatever. What do YOU call it, then?" said Elvis Gold. His frustration and exhaustion made his voice turn raspy.

"I will take you to the place from where my power comes."

Harry Moon looked carefully at Elvis. The illusionist's eyes showed fear, and his skin was as yellow as the shine of his amulet.

"Ah, you admire my alexandrite?"

"I never saw a stone like that before. It's huge."

Elvis unhinged the chain from around his neck and handed it over to Harry to take a closer look. Harry fixed his eyes on the beautiful gem. As he stared at it, the gem turned from yellow to raspberry purple.

"Not everything is magic, Moon," said Elvis Gold. "It is Mother Nature at work. The stone naturally changes in sunlight or candescent light and changes again in candlelight or incandescent light.

"Very pretty," replied Harry Moon.

"It is only nature," affirmed Elvis.

"Not only nature. Nature is the moon and the sea. Nature is beautiful," Harry said as he rolled the amulet in his palm. "Nature, itself, is a stunning mystery and part of the real magic."

The two of them marched up three flights of stairs with Harry Moon leading. They walked together down the corridor of the highest floor and into Harry's bedroom. Elvis Gold smiled to see a poster of himself on the wall. He looked at the various photos of himself which had been torn from magazines and newspapers. His mind strolled down the halls of memory.

147

"Here you are," said Harry Moon.

Harry walked Elvis to a tiny Juniper tree in a green pot by the window. "It is the 'Tree of Life.'"

Elvis Gold stared at the pretty little Bonsai tree.

"So you are a religious kid?" Elvis Gold said with a matter of fact tone. "I heard of this tree. Wouldn't surprise me that you like it."

"To me, it is a symbol of the sacredness of life. I follow the way of the Great Magician."

"And that is exactly who again? Does he have a book or perform?"

"His act left town. When he was here, he did a walking on water bit which was pretty amazing. He actually brought this friend of his back from the dead. But most importantly, he saw all men, women, and children as his friends, all equal in his eyes." Harry looked into Gold's eyes. "Something I don't believe you understand, Mister Gold."

"You know I don't buy that real magic stuff," Elvis Gold said. "I do believe in the love stuff and charity to neighbors, but that's as far as I go."

"That's your free choice. We all are given free choice, Mister Gold. For me, my very life is a magic. From the Great Magician, my magic flows. Your own work too can become more than illusion. But you must want the real magic, Mister Gold."

"I need evidence, Harry Moon."

"What you saw here today is not enough evidence?"

"Only if science could show me such."

"Science is wonderful, Mister Gold. It can tell us much about life. It can reveal the life-cycle of the stars. But science will never show us why we find the stars so beautiful. Mister Gold, you will only know peace when you reach for the fifth element."

"Harry, there are only four elements: earth, wind, fire, and water."

"Magicians know five."

"Then, what is the fifth element, Harry?"

"It is the spirit behind that holds all the other elements together."

"Can I buy some of that from you?" Elvis Gold asked. But there was a smirk on his face. He was only kidding.

Harry ignored the smirk. "I'm afraid not. Mister Gold. It is not for sale. But you can have it for free. Imagine, that the magic that triggered the Big Bang, the magic that created everything from nothing is available to you. When the real magic has its way, Mister Gold, nothing is impossible for you."

But Elvis Gold chose not to believe, even though he could not explain Harry Moon's magic. "Sorry, kid. It's all a slick trick."

"I could not unlock the chains without Rabbit, Mister Gold. But with Rabbit, I can do anything."

"Goodbye, Mr. Moon. I will not forget our time together anytime soon."

Elvis Gold picked up his things and left the Moon home as he came, out the front door.

152

REAL MAGIC

I n the days that followed, Elvis Gold was visited several times by Rabbit in various guises.

In a restaurant in Austin, Texas, Elvis Gold ate the pie, but a bill never came. A waitress behind the counter stood off to the side, smiling.

In Miami, a Santa Claus on a break was pushing through the crowd in Starbucks and stopped long enough to face Gold with sparkling eyes. "Merry Christmas, Mister Gold," said Santa.

In Saint Louis, Missouri, a young girl on the street with sad eyes held out her hat for change. Elvis Gold dropped a ten-dollar bill into her hat. "God bless you," she said. Gold shivered a bit.

No matter what guise he came in, Rabbit seemed to have no noticeable effect on Elvis Gold.

༺ঔৣ༻

One of the wonderful things about life is the people who live it. Harry Moon had met some remarkable people in his young existence. He was always amazed how much he grew from every one of them. Harry even learned from his brother, messy Harvest Moon. Harvest taught Harry how to be patient. His know-it-all sister, Honey, taught Harry how to be tolerant. Elvis

Gold had taught Harry that you need neither fame nor wealth to be rich.

Every night when Harry said the Abracadabra prayer at his bedside, he prayed for Elvis Gold. He prayed that Elvis' hard heart be awakened to the eternal. As Harry traveled through space and time, he thought fondly of Elvis Gold.

It was late afternoon when Mary Moon knocked, opened the door, and walked into Harry's bedroom with the latest distribution of fresh laundry. She carried her earth-tone plastic laundry basket that she had gotten on sale at Target.

"I've washed it, dried it, and pressed it, Harry, but I am not putting it away for you," said Mary Moon. She placed a stack of pants, shirts, and socks on the top of his clothes bureau.

"Thanks, Mom," Harry said as he sat at his desk, working on a code for his computer programming class.

"What's different about the walls of this room?" she asked, looking around.

Harry turned from his homework and looked around the room with his mom.

"Oh, I know," he said with a smile. He had taken down the poster of Elvis Gold.

"What?"

"Your boyfriend."

"My boyfriend?" she asked.

"Your half-naked boyfriend," he replied.

"Oh him," she said, laughing, finally getting it.

"Yes, him."

"But why, Harry? What happened between you and Elvis Gold? You never really told me."

"I dunno," Harry said. "I guess I have just

sort of moved on."

"Good for you. You know what the Book says, don't you?"

"What's that?"

"There comes a time when you have to put away childish things," she replied, as she walked toward the door. She had a few things left in the laundry basket for Honey.

Harry looked up at his mom from the desk.

"Put those clothes away, young man, and I don't mean when hell freezes over, I mean now."

"Yes, ma'am," Harry replied.

Before she left the room, Mary came back to Harry and gave him a kiss on his head.

"What's that for?" he said as he jotted down a code on his scratch draft.

"Just because," she said with a smile. "I am happy you were delivered to my home. I really like living with you." Then she turned, closed the door, and was gone.

Harry was thinking about what his mom had to say. Distracted from his computer programming homework, Harry stood up from his desk.

He walked over to the clothes bureau. He picked through the stack of clothes, pulling out his pants and jeans. He put those into the third drawer where he kept his shorts, sweats, and pants.

"Your mom is right, you know." The voice was Rabbit. Harry turned to find his friend pulling the collared shirts from the stack.

Rabbit strolled across the room with the shirts and put them on hangers in the closet.

"What is Mom right about?" asked Harry.

"About the childish things. When we have

outgrown them, we need to put them away so we can continue to move forward."

Harry sighed. "I feel I am always putting away childish things. First, it was my sandbox trucks, then my crayons, then my early video games."

Always the showman and the ham, Harry grabbed his head in mock distress and said,

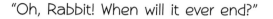

"Oh, Rabbit! When will it ever end?"

Having hung up the two shirts in the closet, Rabbit walked over to the bed and hopped onto the side of it.

"Never," said Rabbit.

"Never?" asked Harry.

"That's the magic thing about life, Harry. We will always be putting things away that once helped us or amused us. That way, we always have room for the upgrades."

"Hmm," Harry said, "I like that."

"However..." said Rabbit.

"However, what?"

"However, we can put away the posters, but we should never put away our friends who are on those posters."

"I wouldn't exactly call Great Gold my friend,"

Harry said. Having finished putting away his clothes, Harry walked over to the bed and sat next to Rabbit.

"Why wouldn't you be a friend to someone who doesn't have many friends?"

Harry scratched his head while he thought about the answer to Rabbit's question.

"He's on tour. He's a zillion miles away in China, I think. He's busy 24/7. He's got five mansions and six Ferraris. He hardly needs me, Rabbit."

"That's exactly why he needs you. As for you, you know that time and space should never get in the way."

"But what can I do besides praying Abracadabra for him at bedtime?"

"You can find ways. There are always ways to reach a friend."

"He's kind of full of himself," replied Harry.

"He doesn't have room for somebody else."

Now Rabbit was getting to the truth.

"Be his friend, anyway."

"He's pompous, too," Harry added.

"Be his friend, anyway."

"He's old. He's like thirty!" Harry further added.

"Be his friend, anyway. You will learn this more completely, Harry, when you fall in love with someone."

"I am in love with Sarah Sinclair! Don't you know anything, Rabbit?" Harry said, somewhat annoyed.

"And what do you say with Sarah? You are always letting her know that you have her back."

"Yeah, that's true, Rabbit. But I really do

have her back. I cannot say the same thing about the back of the Great Gold."

"Man up, Harry Moon," said Rabbit. "Be bigger than you are."

"What would you suggest?"

"Just keep letting him know you are there for him."

"That's not too difficult, I guess," said Harry.

163

"It's harder than you think. You have to remember he's someone you consider arrogant, pompous, and prideful."

"And I don't really like him as a person," added Harry.

"That's why you have to discipline yourself. It's easier to forget people you don't like then to remember them. You have to push on, Harry, to the bigger you. When you turn the other cheek, you are showing not only yourself to be bigger, but you are revealing the magic that is in you.

"Now, be honest, Harry Moon. Don't you wish everyone had a Rabbit?"

164

EPILOGUE

The audience in Taipei, Taiwan was shouting for Elvis Gold's return to the stage. Elvis had already given the audience a spectacular encore, one in which he made a wall of ice cream transform into a polar bear. That was enough. He was at the National Concert Hall in Taipei, the celebrated and grand theater where Rudolf Nureyev had danced and Yo-Yo Ma had played.

It was an honor to perform at the National Concert Hall. Elvis Gold was proud of his global accomplishments. He was considered the world's greatest illusionist and still in his thirties. His world tour had sold out everywhere, and this was his final night in Taipei. Tomorrow, he would be on the plane with the rest of his crew to Paris.

The day after he had visited Harry Moon and his family in Sleepy Hollow, Massachusetts, Elvis Gold began his world tour, and it was now six months since he had been back to America.

Elvis was not quite sure why he was not feeling in a hurry to leave the Concert Hall. He had the strangest sense as if he was not alone in his dressing room. There were bouquets of flowers at the vanity and bottles of celebratory champagne that he would never pop, gifted to him by various dignitaries whom he would never meet. "The tour is lonely sometimes," he thought, "there is so much celebrity and press, and yet I still feel empty."

For some reason which he could not

explain, he sensed that he was not by himself that night in Taipei. He looked through the various cards and tags attached to the flowers and bottles as if he were looking for some special message. But he did not find it among the "best wishes and congratulations" cards. There was no special message.

"Hello?" he said into the air. "Is someone here?"

There was no answer.

161

He began to laugh and thought to himself, "Is Harry Moon's Rabbit here?"

Elvis Gold did not expect an answer from the question in his mind, and he didn't get one.

There was only silence in the room.

Elvis Gold looked into the mirror. He sat down at the vanity and wiped the theatrical make-up from his face with a Kleenex. He forced a smile from his shining, dark eyes.

He placed a few of his personal belongings in his luxury backpack and cocked the bowler hat to the back of his head and smiled. Still, he could not get out of his mind that he was not alone.

"Hello?" he asked a final time as he walked out of the concert dressing room that had been his home for almost a week.

Still, there was no answer.

He walked down the corridor to see the guys from the lighting crew carrying keyboards and electrical patches. He tipped his hat, wishing them good night.

The assistant director, still wearing his ear mike, came up to Elvis.

"Your call time tomorrow is six in the morning," he said.

"Okay," replied Elvis Gold.

"There will be a car waiting for you outside

the front lobby. We should be in the air to Paris by seven."

"Goodnight, then," Elvis said.

Elvis Gold walked out the front door of the Concert Hall. The Hall was still aglow with its signatory evening lights, its mighty pillars of Chinese red, and the blue and yellow rooftop. It was said that there were some three hundred million LED lights that contributed to the magnificent brilliance of the hall at night.

As Elvis walked down the steps and away from the hall, he turned to look at the formidable building one last time. The feeling of not being alone was still with him.

When he adjusted his collar against the wind, Elvis Gold noticed a glimmer. He pulled at his golden collar. He grabbed the chain of his amulet and yanked it up from his chest. The alexandrite gem was glowing emerald. By day, it was gold. By night, it was usually raspberry purple. But now it was glowing green.

In the silence, someone or something seemed to be sending him a message, a message he could not find amidst the champagne bottles or the bouquets of his dressing room.

As Elvis Gold held the glowing amulet in his palm, he turned. It almost seemed as if the wind was pushing him to a different horizon. With the wind at his back, he turned his eyes up from the sidewalk to the brightly lit façade of the Concert Hall.

Before his eyes, the Chinese red pillars lifted up from their pedestals and rearranged themselves into letters. They moved with grace like unseen music moves through the ears of our hearts. The gold and blue filigree from the rooftop fell like rain onto the pillars, conjoining with them in some unique code of wordage.

Elvis Gold pushed the bowler back from his brow so he could see more clearly. Then he saw the red, blue, and yellow letters take shape. He saw an "H" and then an "E." Within moments, the words revealed themselves—

HAVE A MAGICAL LIFE!

Elvis Gold could only smile. As the wind now blew all around, he sensed the aloneness vanishing from his bones. He looked back at the hall, and the pillars of words had reconfigured themselves—

ELVIS GOLD THIS MEANS YOU!

Elvis stood in front of the Concert Hall in awe. He blinked, only to see the message change a third time. This time, it read—

YOUR FRIEND, HARRY MOON

As he looked up at the stars in the sky, Elvis Gold could sense the spaces between them. As he looked to the silhouettes of the few people in the square, he knew, as well, the space between them. Indeed, he knew the people, too. They were part of him. For the first time, Great Gold saw the space around him, not as space, or as an empty land, but as a place rich with life.

Elvis placed the amulet back beneath his collar and pulled the collar up around his neck against the wind. He turned, and continued to walk away from the Concert Hall, and whistled out loud. "Pretty impressive, kid," he thought. "How on earth did you do THAT?!"

Eventually, the night gave way to day. Elvis Gold was ready in the morning when the knock came at the door to make his way to Paris.

M.

174

MARK ANDREW POE

The Adventures of Harry Moon author Mark Andrew Poe never thought about being a children's writer growing up. His dream was to love and care for animals, specifically his friends in the rabbit community.

Along the way, Mark became successful in all sorts of interesting careers. He entered the print and publishing world as a young man and his company did really, really well.

Mark became a popular and nationally sought-after health care advocate for the care and well-being of rabbits.

Years ago, Mark came up with the idea of a story about a young man with a special connection to a world of magic, all revealed through a remarkable rabbit friend. Mark worked on his idea for several years before building a collaborative creative team to help bring his idea to life. And Harry Moon was born.

In 2014, Mark began a multi-book print series project intended to launch *The Adventures of Harry Moon* into the youth marketplace as a hero defined by a love for a magic where love and 'DO NO EVIL' live. Today, Mark continues to work on the many stories of Harry Moon. He lives in suburban Chicago with his wife and his 25 rabbits.

BE SURE TO READ THE CONTINUING AND
AMAZING ADVENTURES OF HARRY MOON

The
AMAZING
Adventures Of

HARRY MOON

Wand - Paper - Scissors

Inspired by true events   Mark Andrew Poe

HARRY MOON is up to his eyeballs in magic in the small town of Sleepy Hollow. His arch enemy, Titus Kligore, has eyes on winning the Annual Scary Talent Show. Harry has a tough job ahead if he is going to steal the crown. He takes a chance on a magical rabbit who introduces him to the deep magic. Harry decides the best way forward is to DO NO EVIL—and the struggle to defeat Titus while winning the affection of the love of his life goes epic.

EVERYONE IS TALKING ABOUT THE ADVENTURES OF HARRY MOON

"After making successful Disney movies like ALADDIN and LITTLE MERMAID, I could never figure out where the magic came from. Now I know: Harry Moon had it all along."

David Kirkpatrick
Former Production Chief, Walt Disney Studios

This may well be one of the most important kid's series in a long time."

- Paul Lewis,
Founder,
Family University
Foundation

"Come on. His name is Harry Moon. How do I not read this?"
- Declan Black
Kid, age 13

"A great coming-of-age book with life principals. Harry Moon is better than Goosebumps and Wimpy Kid. Who'da thunk it?

- Michelle Borquez
Author and Mom

$14.99
ISBN 978-1-943785-00-1
51499>

9 781943 785001

The irrepressible magician of Sleepy Hollow, Harry Moon, sets about to speed up time. Overnight, through some very questionable magic, Harry wishes himself into becoming the high school senior of his dreams. Little did he know that by unleashing time, Harry Moon would come face-to-face with the monster of his worst nightmare. Will Harry find his way home from this supernatural mess?

EVERYONE IS TALKING ABOUT THE ADVENTURES OF HARRY MOON

"Friendship, forgiveness and adventure – Harry Moon will entertain kids and parents alike. My children will have every book in this series on their bookshelf as my gift to them!"

– Regina Jennings
Author and Mom

"Magical and stupendously inspirational, Harry Moon is a hero for the 21st century tween. I wish I had Harry at DISNEY!"

David Kirkpatrick
Former Production Chief, Walt Disney Studios

I can't wait for my next book. Where is the Harry Moon video game?

- Jackson Maison
Kid - age 12

I love my grandchildren and I love Harry Moon. I can't wait to introduce the kids to someone their own age who values life like I do. I hope Harry Moon never ends.

– Scott Hanson
Executive Director, Serve West Dallas and grandpa

$14.99
ISBN 978-1-943785-04-9
51499>

THE
AMAZING
ADVENTURES OF

HARRY MOON

HALLOWEEN NIGHTMARES

Inspired by true events   Mark Andrew Poe

While other kids are out trick-or-treating, eighth-grade magician Harry Moon is flying on a magic cloak named Impenetrable. Harry and Rabbit speed past severed hands, boiling cauldrons and graveyard witching rituals on their way to unravel a decade old curse at the annual Sleepy Hollow Halloween Bonfire. The sinister Mayor Kligore and Oink are in for the fight of their lives.

EVERYONE IS TALKING ABOUT THE ADVENTURES OF HARRY MOON

"When a character like Harry Moon comes along, you see how important a great story can be to a kid growing up."

- Susan Dawson,
Middle School Teacher

"Harry Moon is one wildly magical ride. After making successful films like ALADDIN and LITTLE MERMAID, I wondered where the next hero was coming from Harry Moon has arrived!"

David Kirkpatrick
Former Production Chief, Walt Disney Studios

"A hero with guts who champions truth in the face of great danger. I wish I was thirteen again! If you work with kids, pay attention to Harry Moon."

- Ryan Frank, a Dad and
President, KidzMatter

"This is a book I WANT to read."

- Bailey Black
13-Year Old Kid

$14.99
ISBN 978-1-943785-02-5

51499>

9 781943 785025

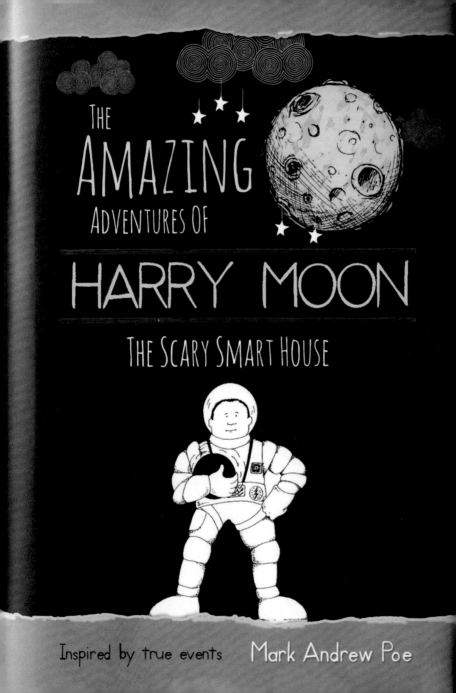

When Harry's sister wins a national essay contest in technology, the whole Moon family is treated to a dream weekend in the ultimate, fully loaded, smart house designed by Marvel Modbot, the Walt Disney of the 21st century. It's an incredible blast, with driverless cars and a virtual reality world. That is, until evil thinking invades the smart technology running the smart house, turning that dream tech weekend into an nightmare! The Moons look to Harry and Rabbit to stop the evil before its too late.

EVERYONE IS TALKING ABOUT THE ADVENTURES OF HARRY MOON

"The Moon family's smart house takes on a bone-tingling dimension when the technology that runs it appears haunted. Say hello to SECOS —a scary Smart Evil Central Operating System!" —David Kirkpatrick, Former Production Chief, Walt Disney Studios

"I'm a grandpa and Harry Moon is a throw-back to the good old days when kids took on wrong and wrestled it to the ground. My grandkids are getting every book."
- Mark Janes, English and Drama Teacher, Grandfather

"If I was stranded on a desert island, I would want a mat, a pillow, a Harry Moon book and a hatchet"
- Charley, KID, age 11

"I pride myself on never making a bad shot. I focus on perfect form and being rock steady. Like me, Harry Moon delivers under pressure. This kid's my hero."
- Jim Burnworth, Extreme Archer, The Outdoor Channel

The new Pizza Slice is doing
booming business, but the kids
in Sleepy Hollow Middle School are
transforming into strange creatures the
more they eat of the haunted cheesy
delicacy. Even the Good Mischief Team
are falling under the spell of the new
haunted pizza slices, putting Harry and
his magic Rabbit on the scent to the
truth behind the peperoni mystery.

EVERYONE IS TALKING ABOUT THE ADVENTURES OF HARRY MOON

"The Moon family's smart house
takes on a bone-tingling dimension
when the technology that runs it
appears haunted. Say hello to SECOS
–a scary Smart Evil Central Operating
System!" –David Kirkpatrick,
Former Production Chief, Walt Disney Studios

"I'm a grandpa and
Harry Moon is a
throw-back to the
good old days when
kids took on wrong
and wrestled it
to the ground. My
grandkids are getting
every book."
- Mark Janes,
English and Drama
Teacher, Grandfather

"If I was stranded on a
desert island, I would
want a mat, a pillow, a
Harry Moon book and a
hatchet"
- Charley, KID, age 11

"I pride myself on never making a
bad shot. I focus on perfect form
and being rock steady. Like me,
Harry Moon delivers under pressure.
This kid's my hero."
- Jim Burnworth, Extreme
Archer, The Outdoor Channel

Hit the trail girls! It's on to the Appalachian Trail. Honey and the Spooky Scouts set off on a mountain trek to earn their final Mummy Mates patch. But an inept troop leader, a flash flood and a campfire catastrophe threaten to keep them from reaching the Sleepy Hollow finish line in time. When all seems lost, Honey Moon takes charge and nothing will stop her from that final patch!

"Honey is a bit of magical beauty...adventure and brains rolled into one."
David Kirkpatrick, Former Production Chief, Walt Disney Studios

"Magic, mystery and a little mayhem. Three things that make a story great. Honey Moon is a great story."
-- Dawn Moore
Life Coach and Educator

"A wonderful experience for girls looking for a new hero. I think her name is Honey Moon." - Nancy Dimes, Teacher & Mom

"I absolutely cannot wait to begin my next adventure with Honey Moon. I love her"
– Carly Wujcik, Kid, age 11

"Charm, wit and even a bit of mystery. Honey Moon is a terrific piece of writing that will keep kids asking for more."
--Priscilla Strapp, Writer, Foster Mom

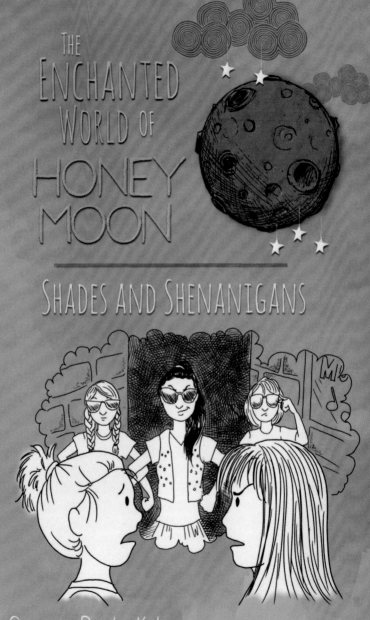

THE
ENCHANTED
WORLD OF
HONEY
MOON

Shades and Shenanigans

Suzanne Brooks Kuhn   Created by Mark Andrew Poe

When Honey comes face-to-face with
Clarice Kligore and her Royal Shades
she knows something must be done to
keep this not very nice club from
taking over Sleepy Hollow Elementary.
Honey sets out to beat them at their
own game by forming her own club,
The Queen Bees. Instead of chasing the
Shades off the playground for good,
Honey learns that being the Queen Bee
is more about the honey than the sting.

"Honey goes where she is needed . . . and everyone needs Honey Moon!"
— David Kirkpatrick, Former Production Chief, Walt Disney Studios

"I wish Honey Moon had been written when
my girls were young. She would have charmed
her way into their hearts."
- Nora Wolfe, Mother of Two

"Heart, humor, age-
appropriate puppy love
and wisdom. Honey's
not perfect but she is
striving to be a good,
strong kid."
— Anne Brighen
Elementary School Teacher

"My favorite character of
all time. I love Honey."
- Elise Rogers, Age 9

"I am a grandmother. I knew ahead of time that these books were
aimed at younger readers but I could not resist and thank goodness
for that! A great kid's book!"
--Carri Zimmerman, Grandmother of Twelve

$14.99
ISBN 978-1-943785-16-2
51499>

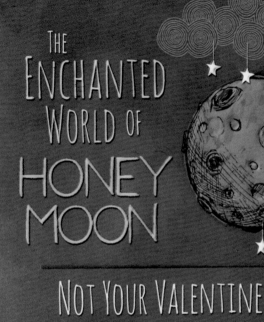

THE
ENCHANTED
WORLD OF
HONEY
MOON

NOT YOUR VALENTINE

Regina Jennings   Created by Mark Andrew Poe

A Sleepy Hollow Valentine's Day dance with a boy! NO WAY, NO HOW is Honey Moon going to a scary sweetheart dance with that Noah kid. But, after being forced to dance together in PE class, word gets around that Honey likes Noah. Now, she has no choice but to stop Valentine's Day in its tracks. Things never go as planned and Honey winds up with the surprise of her Sleepy Hollow life.

"Honey is a breakout wonder... What a pint-sized powerhouse!"
- David Kirkpatrick, Former Production Chief, Walt Disney Studios

"A dance, a boy and Honey Moon - every girl wants to know how this story will end up."
- Deby Less, Mom and Teacher

"What better way to send a daughter off to sleep than knowing she can conquer any problem by doing the right thing."
- Jean Zyskowski
Mom and Office Manager

"I love to read and Honey Moon is my favorite of all!"
- Lilah Black, KID age 8

"Makes me want to have daughters again so they could grow up with Honey Moon. Strong and vulnerable heroines make raising healthy children even more exciting.
--Suzanne Kuhn, Best-selling Author Coach

$14.99
ISBN 978-1-943785-08-7
51499>

9 781943 785087